2

The Story of Peter Cronheim

THE STORY

OF

PETER
CRONHEIM

by Kenneth Ambrose

ILLUSTRATED BY ELISABETH GRANT

DUELL, SLOAN AND PEARCE
New York

First edition

Library of Congress Catalogue Card Number: 62-15476

MANUFACTURED IN THE UNITED STATES OF AMERICA FOR
MEREDITH PRESS

Affiliate of
MEREDITH PRESS
Des Moines & New York

CONTENTS

*This book was written for
Michael and Anthony*

CHAPTER 1

The Birthday Present

Peter was hopping from one leg to the other with impatience. He had been standing by the kerb a full twenty minutes waiting to cross the road to his grandmother's house. Why did she have to live right in the centre of Kolstatt, in a street where every political procession had to pass? And why had this Sunday's march to be such a specially long one?

The police always formed a chain along the route and stopped people from crossing, but on several other Sundays the policeman nearest to where Peter wanted to cross had been kind, and had pretended to look the other way while Peter dashed across in the middle of the procession. Today, on his thirteenth birthday, when he wanted to see his grand- mother even more than on other Sundays, the nearest policeman had just snarled at him, "Get back and wait, sonny."

He kept thinking about the present that had been kept so secret until today. But there was nothing else for it. He stood by the kerb, watching column upon column of uniformed men march past him. Every now and then his boredom was broken by a band; Peter wouldn't have minded so much if there had been more bands. He liked music. But this time they were few and far between, so far apart that you could hardly hear the "Thump-thump, Thump-thump", of the last lot of big drums by the time the next band came around the corner.

He couldn't understand politics at all. He remembered, as he stood there waiting to cross the road, how he came across the word in his father's newspaper when he had just learnt to read.

"Mummy," he had asked, "what is 'politics'?"

"Never mind, darling," Mummy had said. "You won't understand that for a long time."

And now, all he knew was that last week's marchers had worn red ties and this week's were wearing brown shirts; that there were several other kinds, and that sometimes there were fights when two or more of them happened to meet.

It was very puzzling, but there were many more important things to think about as all these people marched past. For instance whether Oma—for that was what he called his grandmother—had his favourite soup for dinner, and whether she had asked any of those boring old friends of hers to afternoon coffee. He certainly hoped it wouldn't be Mrs. Levy again, because she always treated him like a child of six. Nothing annoyed him more than when she limped into the room on her stick and called out, as she always did, "Dear me, hasn't our little Peter grown again! Quite a little man now, aren't we?" After which she would ignore him for the rest of the afternoon and go on endlessly with her uninteresting grown-up talk to his Oma.

At long last the roadway was clear in front of Peter. He dashed across and into the apartment house opposite. It didn't take him many seconds to run up the stairs to the second floor, where his widowed grandmother lived with two of her daughters. Still panting from his rush, he rang the bell on the door marked "M. Cronheim", and then kept his eyes fixed on the little round window in the centre of the door. No one among his family or friends would open the door in answer to a ring before they had looked through this little spy hole to make sure it wasn't another member of the endless procession of beggars or door-to-door salesmen who, his father had explained, were one of the results of Germany having lost the First World War.

A moment later an eye looked briefly through the little window and immediately disappeared again. Peter knew that this was his favourite Aunt Teresa. Anyone else would have opened the door at once, but she was the joker of the family, even though an attack of scarlet fever in her childhood had left her hard of hearing.

"I'm sorry, but we don't want anything today," she called out from the other side of the door, and Peter heard her footsteps going away again. He grinned and banged on the closed door with both his fists for all he was worth. This worked right away. Aunt Teresa came racing back and threw the door open wide.

"All right, all right, Peter, I'm only hard of hearing, not stone deaf. Come along in. Why are you so late?"

"It's that procession down there," Peter said crossly. "I thought it was never going to end."

"And how many times have I told you that everything has an end, except the sausage, and that has two?"

Peter laughed and felt cheerful again. He took off the school cap that looked rather like a station-master's, and his coat. Aunt Teresa hung it up for him, although his mother always said that a boy of his age should do it for himself. Still, she wasn't there to see, and Aunt Teresa wouldn't tell.

His first port of call in the flat was always the kitchen—the second door on the left off the long corridor-like hall.

"Hello, Aunt Lucie, what's for dinner?" he asked as he went in.

"Minced schoolboys with satchel sauce," was the prompt reply from the kitchen, as it had been for more Sundays than Peter could remember.

There had been a time when Oma herself had done all the cooking, and she had always told him with great delight and in full detail what was on the menu. She was still in charge of the household, but now that she was over seventy, Aunt Lucie did most of the cooking. Aunt Lucie's husband had been killed fighting in the First World War, and she did not much like living on her own. So, a few years ago, Oma had suggested that Aunt Lucie should come and live with her and Aunt Teresa, who was not married. Everyone, including Peter, thought this an excellent idea—except of course that Aunt Lucie would never tell him what he was going to have for dinner.

After his brief visit to the kitchen, Peter crossed the hall and opened the dining-room door.

"Hello, Oma, sorry I'm late," he called to the little old

lady in the rocking chair by the window at the far end of the room.

She put down her Sunday paper and said, "Never mind, Peter, I was watching from up here. I didn't think they'd let you through today, seeing that it was a Nazi procession. The police are so friendly with them. I only hope for all your sakes they never get into the government. It doesn't matter to me— I'm too old to care."

"Nonsense, Oma, you may be old, but you're not ancient," said Peter, trying to be a little gentleman. "And in any case I don't see what difference it makes who is in the government. I mean, for ordinary people like us."

"Peter,"—Oma suddenly sounded very serious—"to the Nazis we are not ordinary people. We are Jews, and they hate us. I don't know why, for I'm sure we're no worse than anyone else and a lot better than some."

Peter began to feel uncomfortable. He was out of his depth, so he thought it best to change the subject. "Anyone coming this afternoon, Oma?" he asked.

"No one at all."

He was longing to ask when he could see his birthday present, but with a great effort he forced himself to avoid the subject. After all, he was thirteen now, and he must show his grandmother how grown up he was.

They moved over to the table at the other end of the room and Aunt Lucie brought in the soup. Peter was in luck, because it was his favourite kind: chicken noodle soup, with "fat eyes" floating on top, and the chicken stomach in Peter's plate. And then the other courses were exactly what he would have chosen himself. His Oma and his aunts had made it a real birthday meal. There was chicken and rice with yellow caper sauce. Amazing, Peter thought, how much energy these three women spent on food. There were always special dishes for every member of the family—all the things each one liked best. And more special foods for holidays and birthdays. He loved it, of course, and he was ready to do full justice to the meal in front of him. But he couldn't help wondering what they would do with their time if there were no relatives and if there was no such thing as food.

While Peter was still eating his chicken, he heard a humming noise that grew louder and louder. He jumped off his chair and dashed over to the window.

"An aeroplane!" he called out. "Excuse me a minute."

Aeroplanes were still rare in 1932, and Peter didn't like to miss the sight of one any more than of a fire engine or of the big Zeppelin airships, of which he had only seen two in all his life.

"If you don't sit down, Peter . . ."

Aunt Teresa started to speak, but Peter quickly finished the sentence off for her, because he had heard it so often, ". . . all the food will go straight into my legs, Aunt Teresa, I know. And what's more, I used to believe you when I was little. You know how fat my legs were then!"

The plane had passed over, and Peter sat down again. "It's only one of those little bi-planes," he said in a disappointed voice. "It's flying too high to be interesting and it's not doing any aerobatics."

Aunt Lucie brought in Peter's very best sweet—a chocolate blancmange which really tasted of chocolate and had lots of cream on top. As usual, Peter had two helpings.

"If I eat any more, I'll burst," Aunt Lucie said. "I suppose I'm allowed to say that now?" she added, looking questioningly at Peter. "I remember saying that once when a certain young gentleman was in the room and he was so frightened that he promptly ran outside to wait for the bang."

"All right, Auntie," Peter laughed, "no need to rub it in. I know I wasn't all that brave then, but I'm better now."

When the meal was over and they had all left the table, Peter noticed that the door to the living-room was closed. This was unusual. Normally he walked straight through after dinner and played on Oma's grand piano, which he liked much better than his parents' upright. It was a good time to play the piano, because his aunts were then washing up in the kitchen and didn't have to listen to his mistakes.

"Why is the door shut, Oma?" Peter asked. "Please, may I go in and play the piano?"

"Yes, run along, Peter," Oma replied, and as Peter glanced at her he thought he noticed her exchange a significant look, almost a wink, with her two daughters. Peter wondered whether he was up against another of Aunt Teresa's practical jokes. He remembered the time when their flat was full and he had to be put up for the night in the bathtub. In the morning Aunt Teresa had come in and had woken him by turning on the shower. Well, he thought, it's best to be careful, and he went to open the door to the living-room very cautiously.

He peered in, and suddenly he cried out, "Oh, Oma, a bike! And such a beauty! Oh—thank you, Oma, thank you, Aunt Lucie, thank you, Aunt Teresa! Isn't it a smasher!" With that he turned round and gave each one of them a resounding kiss. He had wanted a bicycle of his own for as long as he could remember, but his father had always said that it would be a waste of money until he was tall enough for a full sized one. So here it was at last. Now he could go out on Sundays with his friends who had bicycles instead of walking in the woods with his parents.

When he had looked at every single part of the bicycle, he sat down at the piano and played Schumann's "Merry

Peasant" twice as loud as usual, though not twice as accurately.

"Poor neighbours, and poor Schumann," said Oma when he had finished. She used to play the piano herself in her younger days so there was no doubt that she knew.

"Never mind Schumann," answered Peter. "He's dead. But I'm glad Fräulein Zopp isn't listening." Fräulein Zopp was his piano teacher. She had gone to school with Peter's mother, but had fallen on hard times when her parents died. The young man she should have married was killed in the

First World War, and ever since then she had been making a modest living by giving piano lessons. Although she was not Jewish herself, she sang in the synagogue choir. If she had been there just then to listen to Peter's playing, she would probably have commented drily, "Well, something like that, but perhaps not quite."

On Sundays at Oma's, if there were no other visitors, much of the afternoon was spent playing either Rummy or Monopoly. Peter was beginning to feel rather bored with Rummy, so today he chose Monopoly—and lost handsomely. Although he didn't like to admit it, he didn't really understand all the buying and selling which is the main part of the game.

"You'll never make a good businessman," said Aunt Lucie, who was a shrewd woman as well as a good cook.

"That's nothing to worry about," Oma said quickly. "Only the Nazis think we are all good at business. Let Peter become a lawyer, like his father, if he wants to."

"Yes, or a teacher," Peter suggested, "but I really hate having anything to do with money."

"Except spending it," Aunt Teresa remarked, smiling.

When dusk fell and it was time to go home, Peter proudly rode his brand new bicycle gingerly along the cobbled streets of Kolstatt. He avoided the tram rails carefully, because it was one thing to get stuck in them and fall off someone else's old borrowed bicycle and quite another to scratch a beautiful new one the first time out.

He soon reached his home, and with much puffing and blowing carried the bicycle up to the second floor of the apartment house where his family lived. It would have been easier to leave the bicycle in the courtyard and put a lock and chain on it, but he didn't feel like leaving his most treasured new possession anywhere except safely behind the

locked front door of his parents' flat. The organ-grinders,
street singers, and even the dustmen who came to the courtyard were his friends. All the same, one couldn't be too
careful.

Later, when his mother said, "Come on, Peter, school
tomorrow; it's time to go to bed," he didn't feel one little bit
tired. He was still far too excited, but he had learnt years ago
that when his parents said "Bedtime" it was no use arguing.
For this reason he had developed his own secret way of obey-
ing his parents and yet, strictly speaking, not doing quite as
he was told. When he had been five or six years old, his father
had bought their first radio, a crystal set with a proper little
cat's whisker and earphones. Peter hated this thing at first,
because sometimes his parents would listen with their earphones on and not hear him call when he was in bed in the
nursery. Then, three years ago, they had bought a loud-
speaker, a brown wooden box with a picture of galleons
woven across the silk cover on the front. Peter hadn't liked
this much at first, either, because when he turned one of the
knobs in front there was sure to be a sudden loud screech
which would frighten the life out of him. However, one
evening, when he was in bed, he had a sudden idea.

The next morning he went to his father. "Please, can I have
your old crystal set by my bed?"

"What, so that you go to sleep even later than you do
now?"

"No, Dad, I'll be much more eager to go to bed, and I
promise I won't listen in too late."

Within the week, the crystal set had been fixed up in his
room, and ever since, if he hadn't felt like going to sleep right
away—well, who could know what time he had fallen asleep
with his earphones on?

So tonight Peter went to bed happily. He had a long

narrow room all to himself. On one side stood the washstand with a bowl and a jug of water, and his wardrobe, from the side of which hung the guitar he was teaching himself to play. At the far end there was a couch under the double glass window that kept the room from getting too cold in winter, even when the outside temperature fell well below freezing point. On the other side of the room were his bed, a chest of drawers and his desk.

To Peter this was not just an ordinary desk. All his treasures were either in it or on it, each one in its special place, and no single soul was allowed to move anything, even in the legitimate business of cleaning the room. There was the little glass dog he had had for so long that he didn't remember where it had come from. There were also the three monkeys sitting in a row and telling him to "Hear no evil, see no evil, and speak no evil". Then he had a place for a large card to which were pinned all the badges he had ever collected, ranging from the German "Lufthansa" airline, via Mercedes cars, right down to his local dairy, where he had once won a competition. Inside one of the deep drawers he kept his collected works: all the drawings he had made over the years, mostly to while away the Sunday afternoons at his Oma's flat when there were boring visitors. Crowning it all were two shelves on which he kept his books in his own exact order, which a librarian might not have recognized at once, but which made it possible for Peter to lay his hands on any one of his books without having to search for it.

Peter turned off the light, jumped into bed, and put on the earphones. He felt snug and he was in no hurry to go to sleep. He listened to a programme of light music, and suddenly he heard a man's voice in the middle of reading the news. Gosh, he thought, I must have dropped off to sleep. Well, it's time anyway. He was just about to take the earphones off, when something the announcer said made him stop and listen a little longer.

This was a news item about the Nazi leader, Herr Hitler, who had made a speech before a record audience in Berlin, in which he had said that the Jews were Germany's great enemy and must be eliminated ruthlessly from German life. What a nonsensical thing to say, Peter thought. He was Jewish, but he had never for one moment considered himself to be anything other than German, certainly not an "enemy of Germany". How could he be? He had never seen any other country. Both his parents and all his grandparents had been born in Germany, his father had been a German soldier in the First World War, and an uncle had been killed in the front line. Being Jewish, as he understood it, was only his religion, and part of the history of long ago.

Then he remembered Oma's words from the morning: "To the Nazis we are not ordinary people. We are Jews, and they hate us." Well, politics or no politics—perhaps it would be better if that man Hitler didn't get into the government.

He took off his earphones and turned over on his side. School tomorrow—have to get up early—pity—must tell them all about my bicycle.

And this was his last conscious thought before he dropped off to sleep.

CHAPTER 2

The Fight

"Peter, you sleepy head, wake up. This is the third time I've called you this morning!"

Peter sat up in bed, but he was still only half conscious, startled awake by his mother's voice. Perhaps this time he had really overslept, and there was nothing he hated more than the thought of being late at school. In a panic, he looked at his watch. It was all right—only a quarter-past seven: if he hurried he would make it in time.

He washed and dressed as quickly as he could, because he preferred to save time on these operations rather than on breakfast. He had only a cup of coffee and a roll before he went to school, but he liked these very much, especially as he could pick his own crusty roll out of the bag that the baker's boy left hanging on the front door knob every morning. He had sorted out the books he wanted and had put them into his satchel the night before, and as soon as he had collected his sandwiches and apple for morning break he was on his way to school.

It was just ten minutes to eight, and school, only five minutes' walk away, started at eight o'clock. That gave him a chance to go over the lessons of the day in his mind as he walked slowly down the road. Or rather, it would have given him the chance on any other morning. On this brisk sunny autumn morning all he could think was, I've got a bicycle, I've got a bicycle, I've got a . . .

"Clang, clang, clang!"

He just managed to jump clear of a tram which was clattering down the only road he had to cross. A narrow escape! If he'd been a second longer dreaming about his bicycle, he might never have ridden it again.

He felt this to be shabby treatment from a tram, because he had always considered trams his special friends. He had "collected" every single tramcar and trailer in Kolstatt, and he even knew when each one had been overhauled last. He had a special weakness for the open-sided trailers that were used on warm summer days. On these you stepped straight from the street into your seat. They gave you a wonderful sensation of travelling at record speed, because there was nothing between you and the road but the arm rest of your seat.

He also had a secret that he had told to no one. When he travelled by tram his favourite place was on the front platform right behind the driver, where he could watch him and the road in front. He had done this so often that he knew exactly how to drive a tram, although he had never in fact touched the controls—unless you counted the time when, in alighting from the front platform, he had accidentally stepped on the bell push, startled a passer-by and earned himself some black looks from the driver. Once or twice he had been tempted to tell someone that he knew how to drive a tram, but each time he had checked at the last moment and said to himself sternly, "No, this is my biggest secret. I won't tell."

The first bell was just ringing as Peter climbed up the dozen or so broad stone steps of the dark building which housed the Goethe Gymnasium, one of the three large secondary schools of his home town. It was named after a German poet, not because there was anything poetic about the place, but because it happened to be in a street of the same name. Once he had passed the statue of Goethe in the sombre entrance hall, Peter always thought the school looked quite bright: the passages were wide and light, though bare, and all the classrooms had large windows.

His own classroom this year was on the ground floor of the four storey building; so he managed to reach it, hang his cap on one of the hooks on the wall, and run over to his desk with a full minute to spare before the second bell rang. This was the bell for silence at two minutes to eight.

"Hello, Rudi," he called out to the boy who shared his desk, "I've got a bicycle!"

"Smashing!" answered Rudi. "Where shall we go on Sunday?"

"Let's go to the Buchwald," Peter whispered, for the eight o'clock bell had just rung and the teacher would be there at any moment.

The Buchwald was a large forest. Most of the trees were tall old beeches and it was full of footpaths and cycle tracks.

Peter often went there on Sundays with his parents, but the idea of going there with Rudi Cohn instead appealed to him much more. They would be able to have adventures in the bushes, climb trees, and pick blackberries to their hearts' content without impatient reminders from grown-ups to "Come along now", and "Do hurry, please!"

Peter loved the Buchwald. It was big enough to get lost in, and yet Peter knew it inside out. At all times of the year there was some attraction: tobogganing in the dead of winter, snowdrops and catkins to find in the early spring, bluebells later, and then wild strawberries, bilberries, redcurrants, blackberries and mushrooms through the summer and autumn. If he and Rudi went next Sunday they would still be in time for the last blackberries and the forest would be bright with colour, in every shade from gold to brown. There would be piles of dead leaves everywhere, and they would make a lovely swishing noise when their bicycles ploughed through them.

There was no time for further discussion, because the door opened and Dr. Hende came in. Everyone stood up, as they always did when a teacher entered. Dr. Hende was their form master, and as teachers went, Peter thought that he wasn't bad. He was tall, young, serious and fair-minded, even though he didn't have a sense of humour. He strode up to his desk in front of the class, faced round and, as usual, said, "Good morning, boys. Sit down."

With a minimum of shuffling and whispering, this order was obeyed. While Dr. Hende checked absences and made his routine entry in the class journal, Peter forced his mind back from his cycle trip in the Buchwald to the English period that was about to start. This was not too hard for him because English was his favourite subject, with French and German drawing for second place.

It didn't seem long to Peter before the bell went again to announce the end of the first period.

"Most unfair," Peter said to Rudi during the five minutes' break between the first two lessons. "Why do periods I like always pass quickly, and the horrid ones I want to see finished go on forever?"

"Don't know," Rudi grumbled. "What's next, anyway?"

That was the one thing about Rudi that Peter didn't like. He always expected Peter to know all the answers instead of looking them up for himself. All the same, there was no doubt in Peter's mind that Rudi was his best friend.

"Silly Latin," Peter found himself saying at the top of his voice, without taking any notice of the Latin master who had just walked in. It didn't matter, because everyone was still talking while they were getting up from their desks. Mr. Senner was never strict, but he loved his boys and they loved him. He came from Southern Germany and spoke in a broad Bavarian dialect, which the boys of this North German town found highly amusing. His large, loose-limbed figure shambled up to the front of the classroom, accompanied by the din from shuffling feet, moving desks, continued conversations, and several hearty calls of "Good morning, sir".

"Better not make so much of a row, boys. Sit down and be quiet." The din quietened down into a hum, but a good deal of activity still went on which Mr. Senner either didn't notice, or chose to ignore. Several boys were called up to translate passages from Julius Caesar. Peter was lucky today. He was left completely undisturbed to carry on, partly in writing and partly whispered, a planning session for his outing with Rudi next Sunday, even down to drawing a map of the projected route. In this way it didn't seem too long until the bell rang again, and they all trooped outside into the school yard with their sandwiches for the main morning break.

The first few minutes of this break usually passed very quietly because most of the boys stood around in groups or squatted on the steps of the school yard, eating the sandwiches, apples, or whatever their mothers had given them. Peter was busy discussing with Rudi the finer points of their planned cycle ride, when they both noticed a scuffle at the other end of the yard.

"Let's go and see what's up," Rudi called out, and they ran across to join the crowd which was growing larger all the time.

"Who is fighting?" Rudi asked Peter.

Just like him, Peter thought; why doesn't he crane his neck

and look instead of asking? Still, he felt charitably inclined towards Rudi at the moment, since they were going to go off on their bicycles together. So he stood on tiptoe to see over the heads of the crowd and called out to Rudi what he saw.

"It's Paul Roth and that horrible Müller boy from the Upper Fifth again. Paul is having a good go at him! And he's only half Müller's size!" Paul was the second of Peter's four friends in class. Rudi Cohn was the best, Paul Roth and Hans Golden were next, and then there was Walter Abel. Peter's parents were friendly with Rudi's, Paul's, and Hans's, and that was probably how the boys all came to be friends in the first place. They had been to each other's birthday parties for as long as they could remember, and, being Jewish, they all met once a week in the afternoon at their religion classes. They also saw each other often on Saturday afternoons at the children's service in the synagogue.

Walter Abel didn't belong to this circle. He was a Christian but he didn't get on very well with some of the other boys in the class, and when there were any quarrels or fights he always sided with the four Jewish boys. Once he had said to Peter, "My dad says that a good Christian is always on the side of the underdog and helps him." Peter didn't really understand what this was all about. A Christian to Peter was simply a boy who went to Scripture lessons during normal school hours, while the Jewish boys had theirs in the afternoon.

The fight wasn't going very well for Paul. The other boy, who was much bigger and was known as a bully, had found himself unable to deal with Paul on his own and had called a couple of his cronies to help him. When Walter Abel saw that it was now three against one, he joined in on Paul's side. Three to two wasn't good enough for the bullies of the Upper Fifth, and two more of them ran up to help.

Now Paul and Walter really seemed to be in trouble. They were hitting out for all they were worth, but with only two of them against five, Peter could see that they weren't going to last many more minutes.

"Come on, Rudi," he shouted, "we'll have to help Paul!"

"It's probably his own fault again," Rudi called back above the din. "He's always opening his big mouth too wide. All the same, let's go!"

They arrived on the scene at the same moment as Hans Golden. The fight went on more equally now, with the five smaller boys managing to keep the five bigger ones at arm's length. Just as Peter thought his side was winning, he heard someone in the crowd shout, "Come on, Upper Fifth, show those Jew-boys where they belong. We'll soon be rid of them!" If there was one thing which roused Peter to a fury it was to be called "Jew-boy". He saw red. His fists suddenly began to hit out at any face on the other side. Before he knew what was happening, he was surrounded by half a dozen big boys. There he was, on the ground, with blows raining down on him and his feet kicking wildly at anything within reach. . . .

"Break this up at once!"

Peter recognized the games master's voice roaring above the confusion. Immediately a lane formed through the circle of spectators, the crowd began to disperse, and the master made his way to the centre of the disturbance where a dozen schoolboys now stood sheepishly waiting to be scolded.

"Now what's it all about, boys?" the games master asked.

"Please, sir," Müller was the first to answer, "Paul Roth called me a thief because I hadn't paid him back the sixpence I borrowed from him last week."

"And so he is," Paul burst out. "He never pays back what he borrows."

"Liar!" shouted the bully, and he was just getting ready for the next round when the games master interfered again.

"Not another word now, or you'll all go up to the Headmaster. Go back to your classrooms at once."

"But they called us 'Jew-boys', sir," Peter said indignantly.

"Never mind that, it takes two to make a quarrel."

With that the games master turned smartly about and went back across the school yard, confident that his last order would be obeyed. And so it was, for everyone in the school knew that he was a reasonable man, but that it didn't pay to cross him.

School finished at one o'clock and Peter ran home, ready as always to eat a big dinner, and none the worse for his fight. However, his mother soon noticed that he had been up to something.

"You'd better go across to Uncle Martin after dinner," she said, "and get him to bandage your knee."

Peter didn't object. Although he disliked having a fuss made of him, he loved visiting his tall stooping doctor uncle with his little goat's beard and deep-set thoughtful eyes. Uncle Martin had married Aunt Katie, one of his father's sisters, and he was the only man apart from his father with whom Peter could hold sensible grown-up conversations.

Sometimes in the summer he would sit with him on his balcony overlooking a quiet square with beautiful old trees, while Aunt Katie was out shopping or was working around the flat. They would talk about plants and animals or how people first came to be on earth, and what made men good or bad, healthy or ill, and how men could all try to become happier by helping each other and being reasonable. This "being reasonable" was a great thing with Uncle Martin. He was always saying how much better life would be if only more people could be made to see reason instead of being allowed to act impulsively and foolishly.

Once Peter had said to him, "It must be very hard to be a doctor and attend to sick people at all hours of the night and day. Do you really like that?"

Uncle Martin had smiled happily and said, "Yes, I do, very much. But that is only half the problem." His expression had become more gloomy as he went on, "All the time we try to make people's bodies better, but we must also try to make their minds better. That is much harder work really. When you have a war like the last one, it makes men hate each other and a lot of good work is wasted. Even now, fourteen years later, many people are still muddled and unhappy, and there is a lot of misery. Sometimes I think things are getting worse, not better."

Poor Uncle Martin, Peter thought. He was always such a pessimist. When other grown-ups said, "Ah well, it'll all come out right in the end," Uncle Martin would shake his head, and his deep melodious voice would take on a tone of sadness as he answered, "Well, I hope so, but I am very much afraid it may not."

"What was the fight about?" Uncle Martin asked Peter with a slight air of amusement as he bandaged his knee.

"Some of the big boys were fighting Paul Roth, and it wasn't fair, so we joined in. I got wild in the end, because some were calling us 'Jew-boys'."

The faint smile immediately disappeared from Uncle Martin's face.

"Didn't you tell the teacher that?"

"Yes, but he said it takes two to make a quarrel."

"So it does, so it does. But still, people should nip anti-Semitism in the bud. It's too horrible to think what might happen if they don't."

"What is anti-Semitism, Uncle Martin?"

"It is people hating Jews for no reason except just because they are Jews."

"You mean like we learn in Jewish History on Wednesday afternoons, where people have sometimes hated the Jews so much that they have killed them or driven them from the country?"

"Yes, I mean just that."

"But surely, that doesn't happen any more?"

"Well, I hope not. People are gradually becoming more educated and enlightened."

Peter could tell from the tone of Uncle Martin's voice that he wasn't really convinced. How hard life must be for a pessimist, Peter reflected, as he wandered back to his flat, proud of his newly earned bandage.

CHAPTER 3

The Election

"What are we going to do next Sunday?" Peter asked at dinner one day towards the end of January. There was plenty of snow on the ground and it looked to Peter as if it might well last over the week-end. "I can't cycle in the snow, but perhaps we can go tobogganing?"

"Not this Sunday, I'm afraid, Peter," said his father. "There is an election for the Reichstag."

"What, another election, Dad?" Peter called out, surprised. "There was one only a few months ago. And always on a Sunday! What is this 'Reichstag', anyway?"

"Well, I suppose it's about time you learnt a little about politics, my boy," his father answered. "From time to time we all go and vote for a party which we should like to see in power to govern the country. The politicians from all the parties for which we have voted then assemble in our Reichstag, and the biggest and strongest parties form the government of Germany. Just lately, each time a government is formed, there are some people who won't obey the law because it isn't their party which is elected. So there has been much disorder, and we have another election to see if we can make the government stronger."

"Dr. Hende said in class the other day that if only the Nazis were elected there would be an end to disorder and there wouldn't need to be any more elections. Do you think that's right, Dad?" Peter asked.

"Yes, because the Nazis would rule by force and make people do whatever they want them to do. I hope it never comes to that, because they hate the Jews, and would make life hard for us."

"Is there nothing we can do to prevent it happening then?"

"Well, Peter, maybe there are one or two things that even young boys like you can do. For instance, it is very important for us that everybody who is not a Nazi goes to vote this time, otherwise the Nazis might well get into power. Our party has asked all those who can find some time on Sunday to go round from door to door and remind our members to vote. I have a list of addresses to go to, but we are very short of helpers. Would you like to have a list as well?"

"Oh, Dad, I'd love one!" Peter could hardly contain his excitement. He had forgotten all about tobogganing in the Buchwald. Surely helping in a grown-ups' election must be so much more fun! "And may I take Rudi with me?"

"I think that would be better than going on your own. You never know whom you might run into. Let's see what Rudi's father thinks about it."

"Please may I phone him, Dad?" Peter pleaded. Until a few weeks ago you had to ask the operator for the number you wanted; now the telephone had a shiny dial which Peter loved, and he never missed a chance to use it.

Rudi's father was just typing out some lists for helpers when Peter phoned him, and he agreed readily to Peter's plan.

"I'll type you out a special little list," he promised, "and I'll give it to Rudi."

"Have you got our list?" was the first thing Peter said to Rudi at school the next morning, even before he remembered to say "Good morning".

"Here it is," Rudi answered. "Dad said not to let anyone at school see it."

Full of the importance of his new secret, Peter folded the list carefully and put it among his school books in his satchel. He didn't dare to look at it again until he was safely out of school.

When he arrived home his mother said to him, "Go and wash your hands; dinner is nearly ready." Five minutes later there was no sign of Peter in the dining-room and no answer when his mother called him. "Peter, whatever are you doing now? Dinner is on the table," his mother said as she put her head round the door to Peter's room. He was kneeling on the floor over a large map of Kolstatt with the list of addresses in one hand. He raised himself up to his full height and looked at her as if he was a member of the government.

"Sorry, Mother, but this is really important. I am studying how I can best help in the elections on Sunday."

"Stuff and nonsense," his mother grumbled. "I told your father that you are much too young to be mixed up in politics. Now come and have your dinner this instant."

The rest of the week seemed to Peter twice as long as usual.

At last Sunday morning arrived and Peter was up early.

"Can I start straight after breakfast?" Peter asked his father.

"No, you must give the people a chance to go voting of their own accord first," his father answered.

More hours of waiting! Peter whiled the time away by poring over the street plan of Kolstatt and following out his route again and again. As soon as dinner was over he ran round the corner to Rudi's flat.

"I've got my electric train out," Rudi said to him. "Let's play a bit first."

"Certainly not," Peter replied sternly. "We have important work to do this afternoon."

"All right then, if we must." Rudi was less thrilled than Peter, but as usual he was willing to follow him.

Ten minutes later they were standing outside No. 5, Bismarckstrasse. Peter's heart started to beat a little faster. He had looked at his list so often during the last few days that he knew by heart the name to look for on the indicator board which was just inside the front door of every apartment house. Even so, he pulled out his list once more and read "M. Bild".

"Come on in," he said to Rudi, and he swept into the hall like an officer leading his troops into battle, with Rudi trailing behind.

They stopped in front of the indicator board. Yes, there it was: "2nd Floor—R. Solt
                           M. Bild"

They rushed up the first flight of stairs. Then a little more slowly up the second flight. When they arrived at the top of the stairs Peter's heart was pounding away, partly with the effort and partly with excitement.

"Let's wait a minute," Peter said. "I'm out of breath."

"Scared?" Rudi asked, with a malicious twinkle in his eye.

"Of course not," Peter answered, but right deep down inside at this moment he would have been quite glad if someone had said to him at this moment that the election was called off and they should both go home.

"You remember what we have to say?" Rudi asked.

"Excuse me, sir or madam," Peter intoned, "we are helpers of the Democratic State Party. Would you kindly tell us whether you have voted yet, please?"

"Right," said Rudi, "I'll ring." He put his finger on the bell push—but no sound came out of it.

"Push harder," Peter ordered.

Rudi did, but the bell was still silent.

"Can you hear anyone inside?" Peter asked.

Rudi put his ear to the letter box. "Not a sound," he said.

Peter could feel his excitement flow out of him, just as if it was his bathwater and someone had pulled out the plug.

"Not a very good start," Rudi added.

Why must he rub it in, Peter thought, but putting on his officer air again he said aloud, "Well, there are plenty more names on our list. We must get on."

Their next call was a few houses farther down. It was a Mrs. Sonntag, who lived on the first floor. Peter was less excited now. His first failure had broken the tension which had been mounting during the last few days.

This time the bell worked. An elderly lady opened the door. She had a stick in one hand and an ear-trumpet in the other. "Y-e-e-s?" she said and put the trumpet to her ear.

Peter stepped up close and recited his little piece exactly as he had practised it during the last few days, only a little louder.

"No, I'm not voting any more. I'm getting past it. But come in a minute and I'll make you a nice hot cup of coffee. It's cold out today, isn't it?"

"Thank you very much, Mrs. Sonntag, but we really must get on," Peter said hastily, and he pulled Rudi along with him down the stairs, even before the old lady had shut the door.

At the next address—it was on the fourth floor, and there was no lift—a young man came to the door and said he had already voted, thank you very much. After this, Peter was grateful to have a ground floor flat on his list. Rudi was by now the confirmed bell-ringer, and a few seconds after he had rung, there was a shuffling of slippered feet on the other side of the door. The middle-aged man who opened it looked as if he had just been woken up.

"Isn't there any peace to have a nap even on a Sunday afternoon?" he grumbled. "What d'you want, you two?"

This put Peter off his stroke. In al   practising he hadn't thought of the possibility that he might wake someone up. However, he quickly collected his wits and said as apologetically as he could, "I do beg your pardon for disturbing you, sir, but we are helpers of the Democratic State Party. Would you kindly tell us whether you have voted yet, please?"

"What, today?" the man said, looking at them in surprise. "Aren't the elections next Sunday?"

"No, sir, it's today," Peter said, full of importance now, "and every vote is needed, please."

"Well, fancy that." The man laughed. "I'm so glad you came, sonny. I would have missed it otherwise. I would have looked a fine sight next week, turning out for an election that was held the week before, wouldn't I?" And he broke into a

"What, today?" the man said, looking at them in surprise.

fit of hearty laughter at the thought of his one-man election on the following Sunday. "I'll go right now, just let me put my shoes and coat on. You're quite right, we must all go, otherwise those Nazi fellows may yet get into power."

"Thank you very much, sir, and good-bye," Peter said, and started towards the street. This time, however, he wasn't really walking, he felt as if he was floating on air. He could have burst with pride at the thought that now he had actually swelled the votes of his father's party by one.

As the afternoon wore on, he and Rudi had a few more successes. They were mostly people who wanted that little extra push or reminder to take the trouble to vote. There were also a couple more embarrassments. One lady said she thought little children should be kept indoors on election day, and one man told them to mind their own business. Twice they both took fright and ran off: once when a householder opened his door and a big Alsatian shot out and barked at them in a most unfriendly manner, and the other time when they discovered to their horror that a man who had been included on the list turned out to be a Nazi Party member.

It was nearly dark by the time they had finished their round and returned to Rudi's flat. Rudi's father opened the door to them.

"Well," he asked, "how did it go?"

"It was ever so exciting," Peter said breathlessly. "Please may we go again at the next election?"

Rudi's father smiled. "Let's hope we get the government we want, and that there won't be another election for some time," he said. "What about coming inside now for some coffee and cake with all the other helpers?"

He opened the door to the sitting-room, and Peter started back with surprise. He had been too excited to notice the

noise behind the closed sitting-room door, but now he saw
that the room was packed with people eating and drinking
and the air was thick with cigar smoke. They were all telling
each other their experiences, until Rudi's father called out
above the din, "One moment, please! I want you to meet
Peter and Rudi, our two youngest helpers."

The hush only lasted a moment. Almost immediately
Peter and Rudi were in the centre of a circle of grown-ups,
all saying "Oooh!" and "Aaaah!" and "Well done!" and
wanting to hear their story.

Well, Peter thought, as he munched the huge piece of cake
someone had pushed into his hand, perhaps politics are not so
hard to understand after all. To him at this moment it
certainly meant coffee and cake and being a little hero and
the centre of attention. While he recounted his successes and
his mishaps of the afternoon time and time again, he felt that,
taken by and large, his little anxieties had been worth it,
because for the first time in his life he had really achieved
success in the world of adults.

It was evening by the time Peter reached his own home
again. All through supper Peter repeated his afternoon
adventures to his parents. Then, as bedtime arrived, he
pleaded, "Please, Dad, may I stay up a little longer just for
once to listen to the election results on the radio? I do so
want to know who won!"

"Well," his father answered quickly, before his mother
was able to say "No," — "as you did such a grown-up job of
work this afternoon, you can come over to Oma's flat with
us now, and we'll all listen together."

They dressed warmly and went out into the clear cold
winter evening. The streets were quiet now, and the snow
made its familiar crunching noise underfoot. The street
lamps were far apart, and in between them it was dark enough

for Peter to see thousands of stars twinkling in the black sky above. Peter felt on top of the world. He loved weather like this and he was pleased to be allowed to stay up late and be admitted as an equal to a real grown-ups' evening. He was quite certain that with all his efforts that afternoon and the work done by all the other helpers whom he had met in Rudi's flat the election results would favour his father's party and go against the Nazis. In his mind the whole election was like a sports contest at school: if you worked and played hard you were most likely to win.

Five minutes later, they entered Oma's sitting-room.

"Well, I never——!" Oma exclaimed when she saw Peter. "Since when have you been interested in election results?"

"Since this afternoon when I worked as a helper for the Democratic State Party, Oma," Peter answered proudly.

"Did you really?" said Oma, surprised. "You must be cold and tired. Do sit on this chair nearest to the stove."

The stove was big and rectangular; it filled a whole corner of the room from the floor nearly up to the ceiling. Its plain white tiles were broken only by two iron doors: one at the bottom to put the coal in and take the ashes out, and one half-way up. This second door held a special interest for Peter. Behind it was a compartment which was so hot when the stove was on that you could bake apples in it. Luckily for Peter, it was almost in constant use in Oma's house in the winter.

"I'm not quite sure how grown-up you are tonight," Aunt Teresa said to Peter when he had sat down. "We are having red wine and biscuits, but I think by pure chance there happens to be a baked apple in the stove."

"I think I'd still like that better than wine, thank you," Peter answered, putting his pride firmly behind him for a moment. While the grown-ups were filling their glasses,

Peter covered his baked apple with sugar and tucked in heartily, forgetting for the moment why he had come to Oma's this evening.

The door bell rang again. Aunt Lucie went out and returned presently with Uncle Martin and Aunt Katie. For the next quarter of an hour, Peter was the centre of the party again, as he had to tell his story in every detail to the assembled family. When he had finished, Uncle Martin said, "The first results ought to be announced soon."

Before anyone else had a chance, Peter jumped up and switched the radio on. In a few seconds the music of a military band drowned all conversation.

"Good Heavens, Peter, not so loud," Aunt Teresa shouted. "This set is only intended for us, not for the neighbours' flat. They have one of their own."

Peter turned the set down and went back to his place near the stove. This wasn't the first time he had heard election results on the radio. After some of the last few elections he had gone to bed, put his earphones on as usual, and listened to the programmes for a while. They had always been musical programmes, and he well remembered being irritated by the frequent interruptions which started, "We are now able to give you the following election results . . ." The details which followed had been meaningless to him, and he had usually taken off his earphones fairly early on election nights.

Tonight it was the other way round. He could hardly wait for the music to stop so that he might find out how his efforts during the afternoon had helped. Quite soon the music faded out. The conversation in Oma's room stopped suddenly, except for Aunt Teresa who, being slightly deaf, hadn't heard the music go quiet. ". . . and I told him just what he could do with his bananas at that price . . ." she was saying to Aunt Katie at the top of her voice, before she noticed that everyone else had stopped talking and was looking towards the radio. "Oh, sorry," she said awkwardly, "is it starting?"

"We now interrupt this programme of military music," said the announcer's voice, "to give you the first election results. Hamfurt North:

National Socialists	37,356
Communists	31,212
National Party	12,105
German Centre Party	8,754 . . ."

The voice went on for ages, it seemed to Peter, reeling off the names of strange parties and the number of votes, which were becoming smaller and smaller. Suddenly Peter heard a familiar name:

". . . Democratic State Party, 1,289 . . ."

"Oh," Peter said, disappointed, "is that all? I thought . . ."

"Shh," interrupted Uncle Martin, "let's hear the rest."

As Peter glanced across at him, he thought Uncle Martin looked more worried and anxious than he had ever seen him before.

The music started up again, and so did the conversation in the room.

"What's the matter, Uncle Martin?" Peter asked. Uncle Martin had not taken his eyes off the radio when the announcer finished and did not seem conscious of the other people in the room. Peter's question woke him out of a dream.

"What's the matter?" he repeated. "Oh—nothing really, I was only thinking that this result isn't a very good beginning."

"We'll never change you, Martin," Peter's father joined in. "Always the pessimist. Just because the first of a few hundred results doesn't suit us, you think it's the end of the world."

"I wish I could feel as happy as you do about this election," Uncle Martin answered.

Presently, the music stopped again, and so did the talk in Oma's sitting-room. Two more results were about to be announced. Surely, Peter thought, this time they would be more favourable to "his" party.

". . . National Socialists, 25,784 . . ."

Peter's heart sank. The Nazis were top again! Still, maybe "his" party was next?

". . . National Party, 21,063 . . ."

Maybe the Democratic State Party was third, then?

". . . Communists, 12,980 . . ."

The announcer's voice went on like a robot which you could start but then couldn't stop however hard you tried:

". . . German Centre Party, 9,137 . . ."

Please, Peter thought to himself, please, Mr. Announcer, say my party next. But the announcer went on with his list for another age, before he said,

". . . Democratic State Party, 917 . . ."

The second of the two results was similar, and Peter was beginning to feel quite downhearted. What if Uncle Martin was right after all, and the National Socialists, whom they all called the "Nazis", won the election? Peter had enjoyed his part in the game so far, but if his side lost, what would happen?

Just then, as if he had heard the question in Peter's head, Uncle Martin said, "If the Nazis win, we may as well all write our last will and testament."

"Nonsense, Martin," argued Aunt Teresa. "If they form a government they'll be able to examine us and find out that we haven't any horns or tails like so many devils, and then they'll have to pass a law which says that Jews are just like all the other Germans, only different."

Aunt Teresa knew how to make everyone laugh; even Uncle Martin managed a smile at her last funny remark, only Peter was not quite satisfied. He could hardly wait to hear the Kolstatt result. He was quite sure in his own mind that the Nazis couldn't have won in his own home town, however well they might have done elsewhere.

During the next half-hour most of the results fell into the same pattern. There was the occasional one where the Centre Party or the National Party were at the top, and each of these results was greeted in Oma's sitting-room with a chorus of "There you are", and "Good", and "You see, it's not so bad as all that!"

"Let's go home," Peter's father said after a while, "Peter has to go to school tomorrow."

"Oh please, Dad," Peter pleaded, "may we just stay until they announce the Kolstatt result?"

"All right then, if it comes on soon."

Just for once this evening, Peter was lucky. They were only half-listening to the next batch of results, when suddenly Peter heard,

". . . Kolstatt—National Socialists, 30,146 . . ."

"Oh, blast!" Peter burst out, without listening to the rest of the result. He could have cried, he was so disappointed. He wouldn't have minded if the Nazis had been top in every other result in Germany. But in his very own Kolstatt, where he had tried so hard to help the others to win—this was more than he could easily bear. He swallowed hard. He mustn't let the others see how near he was to crying, so he dashed outside into the hall and put his coat on.

"That's enough of elections for me," he said as he came back into the room carrying his parents' coats. "Let's go home now. Thank you very much for having me, Oma."

"You shouldn't have let the boy help with the election,"

Oma said to Peter's father. "Look how upset he is now. He would have learnt about politics soon enough."

"I don't agree," answered Peter's father. "It looks as if Martin is right for once, and the Nazis have really won this time. We Jews will feel politics in our daily lives at any moment. So the sooner our children learn about it the better."

As they trudged back silently through the snow, Peter suddenly asked, "Dad, do you think I ought to fight Müller at school tomorrow to show him I don't care whether his side won the election or not?"

"I should let sleeping dogs lie," said his father firmly.

"And don't you start anything," his mother added quickly. "There are a lot of Nazis and only a few of us, and it looks as if we'll have to live with them for a long time."

CHAPTER 4

Peter's World Changes

For some time after the election things seemed to Peter to go on very much as usual. The hateful boys at school, like Müller, were still hateful, and the decent ones were still friendly. There were just a few who no longer said "Good morning" to Peter, but these were mostly boys he hadn't liked anyway. When the teachers entered the classroom, they said "Heil Hitler" instead of "Good morning" but the boys made just as much or as little noise as they had done before.

Among the teachers, Dr. Hende was as fair and as humourless as usual, but Peter thought he looked just a little more proud. Mr. Senner, on the other hand, had become more irritable and nervous. Sometimes he would just stare into space for a few moments, like someone who has something on his mind.

Perhaps Uncle Martin was wrong after all, Peter thought. Things don't seem bad, really. Maybe the lost election was not as tragic as some grown-ups thought.

Then suddenly, in the spring, things began to happen.

All the year round, Peter didn't read the newspapers. Once a year, however, he always did: this was on April the first, when he had lots of fun trying to sift out the ordinary news from the "April Fool" items which all the German papers printed on that day.

On this April Fools' Day in 1933 he dressed as quickly as he could and then ran to the front door to collect his roll and the *Kolstatt Daily Journal*. He wandered back to the dining-room studying the headlines. "Ouch!" he cried out, as he bumped into a chair which he hadn't noticed because he was too busy reading. But he forgot about his bump immediately, for there, right on the first page, he read:

Space Flight Attempt

"Prof. N.O.N. Sense of the University of Increditon, U.S.A., hopes to make the first attempt at space flight today. After studying weather charts for all parts of the world, he has decided that the most favourable time and place for launching his one-man rocket will be this morning at 11 a.m. from the centre of Kolstatt, and he has chosen the Kaiser Wilhelm Memorial Square for his take-off. We are delighted that our town has been selected for this historic event, and it is hoped that the whole population will turn out to greet the professor."

Obvious, Peter thought. How could anyone be expected to fall for that one? He went on scanning the pages, and in a moment or two came across this item:

Progress in Trams

"A new kind of tram which can be converted into a boat has been developed by the Kolstatt Transport Department. A demonstration of this new amphibious vehicle will be given by the River Koll at 12 noon today. The first twenty persons on the site will be given a free trial run along and on the river."

Can't fool me with that one either, Peter thought; and read on:

A Reminder

"All citizens of Kolstatt are reminded that April 1st 1933 must go down into history as 'Boycott Day'. Let everyone show today that he or she is a good German. Let us boycott all Jewish shops, restaurants and other institutions. Do not consult Jewish doctors or lawyers. Keep Germany Aryan and free from Jewish influence!"

Surely, Peter thought, this cannot be an April Fool. And yet it seemed too mad to be real. He ran to his parents' bedroom.

"Dad," he said, "look what it says here in the *Journal*. They can't mean that, can they?"

"I am afraid they can and they do," said his father quietly. Peter noticed that he was making an effort not to look too worried.

"Is there anything I can do to help, as I did at the election, Dad?" Peter asked.

"Sorry, Peter, it's too late. We can't do anything now until the government changes again. Meanwhile we'll just have to grin and bear what comes. It may not turn out too badly. Just make sure you keep out of trouble on your way to and from school today. If you see any crowds, keep well away."

Peter went to school with a heavy heart. On the way he passed the delicatessen shop which belonged to Paul Roth's father. He noticed in front of it a burly man wearing the Nazi Brownshirts' uniform. He was holding a big placard, and on it Peter read:

"JEWISH SHOP
GOOD GERMANS DON'T
SHOP HERE"

His heart beat faster than usual, and his face flushed with rage, but he remembered his father's advice about keeping out of trouble, and crossed over to the other side of the road.

"Did you see what's happening outside your shop?" Peter said to Paul Roth during break at school.

"Of course I did," Paul answered, full of self-confidence as always. "Won't do them any good. They're wasting their time. The League of Nations won't allow them to do us any real harm."

"What's the League of Nations?" Peter asked.

"Don't know, really," Paul admitted. "But anyway, that's what my dad says."

Walter Abel came up just in time to catch the last few words. "My dad says that we must continue to do the right thing whatever happens," he said. "It doesn't matter whether a shopkeeper is Jewish or Aryan. But it matters whether he is a good, honest shopkeeper or not."

On the way he passed the delicatessen shop. . . .

When Peter went home from school that day, there was another Brownshirt in front of the Roths' shop holding up the same placard.

I wonder whether it will get any worse, Peter thought. He didn't have to wait long for the answer.

A few days later, when he came home from school, his mother said, "We're going to have dinner without Dad today. He told me we shouldn't wait for him."

"Why?" Peter asked. "Is Dad staying in court? Has he another one of those exciting cases where the jury can't make up its mind?"

"I wish he had," his mother sighed. "No, Peter, you may as well know that the Nazis are about to pass a law forbidding Jews to practise as lawyers, except among their own fellow-Jews. That means most of them, and probably your father, will have no work. He has gone out to arrange a meeting of all the Jewish lawyers of Kolstatt so that they can discuss what to do."

"But, Mother, this seems all quite senseless," Peter said. "All Dad's clients always say what a good lawyer he is and how he has helped them. And surely, if he can't practise any more, he can't earn any money, can he?"

Peter was puzzled and worried. He looked at his mother and noticed that she was worried too.

"No, I'm afraid he won't earn much now," she answered. "We'll be very short of money for a while, but I expect we'll manage somehow."

"I wish I was big enough to earn some money," Peter said. Then suddenly an idea struck him, and he added, "—but if we are really very hard up, I can always sell my bicycle."

"It's very good of you to offer," his mother said quickly. Peter noticed that she had to swallow hard before she continued, "But I do hope we won't need to ask you to do that."

Just then the telephone rang, and Peter ran to see who it was.

"Dad here, Peter," said the voice at the other end. "I'm in rather a hurry. Would you tell Mother I shan't be home until the early evening, and that I'm asking about fourteen people to come over to our flat at eight tonight?"

"All right, Dad. Any other news?"

"Nothing now. Bye-bye."

"Bye-bye, Dad, see you later."

"Fourteen people!" his mother said. "He must be holding a meeting of all the Jewish lawyers here tonight."

"Then why didn't he say so?" Peter asked.

"Because these days you have to be very careful what you say on the telephone. The Nazis are getting people to listen to telephone conversations, and if they thought there was a meeting being held here, they might think it something political and arrest the lot of us. But mind you don't say anything to anyone about telephones being tapped. The Nazis don't like that."

In the evening, from about ten minutes to eight onwards, the door bell rang every few minutes. Peter had been allowed to open the door to the visitors and he enjoyed that because it made him feel that he was doing something useful in the world of grown-ups. The guests seemed to him pale and anxious, even though most of them managed to say a friendly word to him as they came in, and some even inquired how he was getting on in school. But then they all hurried into the sitting-room, which tonight was "out of bounds" for him and his mother. Rudi's father, who was a lawyer like Peter's, arrived last of all. Peter noticed how sad he looked compared to the last time he had seen him on election day. He seemed ten years older tonight.

Peter went to bed as soon as Rudi's father had gone inside.

He switched off his light but he couldn't sleep. He heard snatches of the lawyers' discussions from the living-room across the hall, and he strained to listen.

". . . but Ex-Servicemen will still be able to practise," one of them said.

"I shouldn't dream of taking advantage of my war service to score against my friends and colleagues," he heard his father say. "We swim or sink together . . ."

Peter lost the thread of the argument again, as several of them were speaking together.

". . . and we must ask our friends who have businesses to help find us employment . . ." said another voice.

"In any case we'll have to tighten our belts. We don't know how long this will go on, and you can't eat up all your . . ."

"I keep telling you," another voice interrupted, "the only real solution is to emigrate at once if you possibly can. There's no sense in waiting for the worst to happen."

"Now please, gentlemen," Peter's father said, "don't let's panic."

"I tell you," the other voice said again, "it's not a question of panicking, it's common sense. Let's get out of this country while it's still possible, even if we have to leave all our possessions behind. At least we can save our lives and those of our families."

"I couldn't live in any other country," someone else said, and Peter thought he recognized the voice of Rudi's father, only it sounded much quieter and sadder than usual.

"At least send your children out of the country, if you won't go yourself," the first voice insisted.

"Yes, but where?" someone asked.

Then the conversation got jumbled again, and Peter couldn't follow it any more. Besides he was getting more and more tired. Some phrases kept going round in his head:

". . . get out while it's still possible . . . at least send your children out of the country . . . yes, but where? . . . get out . . . where? . . . must tighten our belts . . . don't panic . . ."

And so he dropped off to a restless sleep.

When Peter had finished his homework on the next afternoon, his mother gave him a postcard and said, "Please run round the corner with this, to the offices of the *Kolstatt Daily Journal*, Peter."

"All right, Mother," Peter answered, and he turned the card over to see what was written on it. He read:

"Classified Advertisements.

ROOM TO LET
Bright large bed-sitting-room to let in quiet
household near town centre. Phone 20805."

"Are we going to let a room in our flat, Mother?" Peter asked.

"Yes, Peter," answered his mother. "I expect you gathered yesterday that your father is not going to have much work for some time and we are going to be hard put to it to make ends meet. So we decided to let a room and use the money we get from it to help with the rent."

"Well, I hope we'll get someone nice to live with us," Peter said, "then we won't mind so much, will we?" And off he went to deliver the card.

Every morning after that he studied the classified advertisements in the paper while he was eating his breakfast roll. It wasn't until the fifth morning after he had been to the office with the card that he found it. He didn't concentrate on his lessons that day, but kept on wondering what kind of a lodger he would find when he arrived home for dinner.

As soon as he was inside the door, he asked his mother, "Well, who've we taken?"

"It isn't that easy, Peter," his mother answered. "Two or three people came along, but when they found out this was a Jewish household they all said they'd think about it and let us know. You know what that means, don't you? We won't see them again. There was only one who seemed really interested and he'll probably come back."

"Who was that, Mother?"

"Well, his name was Schulz, and he said he had a lot of Jewish friends. He's a tram driver."

"A tram driver!" Peter was beside himself with excitement. He had never dreamt that he might have a real tram driver living in his very flat. "Oh, Mother, I do hope he comes back. You'll take him if he does, won't you?"

"I think so," said his mother. "He seemed a nice enough gentleman."

A week later, Herr Schulz moved in. He didn't have many belongings, but he made a great fuss over his radio set. He said radio was his hobby and asked whether he could lay his aerial wire under the carpet right across the hall. Peter's mother didn't really like that, as she thought it wouldn't do the carpet much good, but as Herr Schulz seemed such a nice modest little man, she let him do it.

Peter was delighted with the lodger. Whenever he could think of a pretext, he would knock on his door. Herr Schulz would come to the door, Peter would deliver his message, or ask his question, and then try and start a conversation about trams. Herr Schulz was very patient and good-tempered, and he seemed to like Peter well enough. Yet sometimes Peter wondered why Herr Schulz never asked him inside his room. Perhaps he just doesn't like snoopers, Peter thought, so he carried on his talks standing on one side of the door and

Herr Schulz on the other. At times, too, Peter thought that, for a tram driver, Herr Schulz ought to know more about trams than he did. If Peter caught him out with a question he couldn't answer, Herr Schulz would smile and say, "Well, of course I only drive the things, I'm not married to them or the Transport Department."

Shall I tell my secret to him? Peter wondered. What would he say if he knew I could drive a tram, too? Well, perhaps I'll wait a while till I know him better. And so he still kept his big secret to himself.

April gave way to May. Peter loved this month. He liked the new green on the trees, the wealth of flowers blossoming in all the window boxes and public squares, and the sun shining really hot for the first time. The cycle tracks in the Buchwald had dried up and made easy going for his bicycle which was still shiny and new looking, as he had not been able to use it much in the winter.

Above all he was glad that the steamers had started their regular service to the seaside again. In a three-hour trip they took you right to the Baltic Sea with its miles of wide golden sandy beach. Aunt Teresa had a season ticket on the steamers in summer and would go to the seaside every Sunday morning early and come back after dark in the evening. Sometimes she would take Peter and then they had a lovely time burying each other in the warm sand, splashing about in the water, and talking to the seamen on the boat. Aunt Teresa knew them all, from the captain downwards, and for a special treat the captain let them come on to the bridge once or twice each season.

One morning in May Peter arrived in his classroom to find Rudi's seat next to him empty. It was unusual for Rudi to be late, and even more unusual for him to miss school for anything except his regular annual cold, which he almost always had in October or November. Throughout the morning Peter waited for Rudi to turn up, but school finished and Rudi still hadn't come.

Peter ran home as fast as he could. His mother and father were both at home when he arrived.

"Rudi wasn't at school today," Peter said, "and besides . . ." He stopped abruptly, when he saw his parents' faces. He had never seen them like that before. They were dreadfully pale and their eyes were full of compassion.

"What's the matter?" Peter said, frightened.

"You'll have to know sooner or later, so you may as well know now," Peter's father said in a voice which had lost all its usual liveliness. "You'll never see Rudi or any of his family again."

"Why? Have they gone away, or been imprisoned or something?"

"No, Peter," said his father, "they have left us for ever. They all died last night, peacefully, in their sleep."

Peter felt his legs give way under him, and dropped into the nearest chair. He wanted to ask another ten questions, but he felt as if someone had his hand round his throat, and however hard he swallowed he couldn't get a word out. His mother moved over to him and put a protective arm round his shoulder.

"It's all terribly, terribly sad," she said with an unsteady voice. "Have a good cry, if you feel like it."

Poor Peter didn't need any encouragement. He burst into tears, and gradually he found the hand round his throat loosening its grip.

"How . . ." he managed to ask at last, "how did it happen?"

His mother went out to the kitchen and returned with a mug full of hot cocoa. "Drink this," she said, "it'll do you good. Dad will tell you what happened."

Peter's father cleared his throat. "You see, Peter," he started, "Rudi's father felt much more strongly than I do that the arrival of the Nazis means the end of the Jews in this country. He thought that our lives here would become more and more wretched, until the Nazis would finally make good their threat to rid Germany of all Jews. He believed that there were only two ways out: either to leave Germany, which he didn't want to do because he loved his country and couldn't live anywhere else; or to kill himself and his family so that they should have peace and not lead lives of misery here. So, when everyone was soundly asleep, he closed all the windows, turned on the gas and went back into bed. This morning the neighbours found them all dead."

"Do you think he did right?" Peter asked, dazed from the dreadful news.

"In a situation like this," his father answered, "everyone

has to make his own decision. I cannot judge poor Rudi's father. All I know is that I see things differently. I think that the children and young people ought to try and start a new life in other countries, and if matters become much worse here, then your mother and I will also try to emigrate. Meanwhile we've written to one or two friends abroad and asked if they could find a school for you and look after you."

Peter felt his temper rising. "I won't go!" he shouted at his parents. "Why should I have to be pushed out on my own? I've done nothing wrong! I hate the Germans, and I hate you! You're trying to get rid of me, that's all! Well you're not going to!"

He ran to his room before his parents could say anything and banged the door after him. He threw himself on his bed and buried his head in his pillow. "They're trying to get rid of me," he sobbed. "I hate them, I hate them, I hate them. I won't go, not ever!"

The door opened quietly, and he knew without looking that his mother had entered the room. She sat down on the edge of his bed and started to stroke his hair. Gradually Peter felt his rage leaving him, and there remained only a dull feeling of pain at the loss of his best friend.

"Now please don't upset yourself so much," his mother said. "Things may get better here, or we may yet all leave together. Dad and I will never 'push you out', as you said just now, unless you want to go. And that's a promise!"

"Now let's go and have some dinner," Peter's father said from the other side of the door, trying to make things appear as normal as possible.

Peter couldn't have said what he was eating that day. He wasn't thinking about food but about poor Rudi and his family, and about himself in a strange country and without his parents.

CHAPTER 5

The Seaside

It took Peter a long time to get used to school without Rudi. Everything seemed just that little bit duller than usual because his best friend wasn't there to discuss it with him. He didn't even look forward to the annual school camp at Henkendorf, which before he had always loved better than anything else in the school calendar.

Henkendorf was a village by the Baltic, away from all the fashionable resorts, but with a beach as wide and golden as anywhere else along that coast. Peter's school maintained a permanent Home there, and every summer two or three classes at a time went for a fortnight during term time to have a minimum of lessons, and a maximum of fresh air and fun. When Peter's parents heard that it was to be

Peter's class next, they were delighted, for they thought it might help to cheer him up.

"Aren't you looking forward to going to Henkendorf?" his mother asked.

"I suppose I am," Peter answered. "I am not too keen on the early morning run down to the beach, but I do like it by the sea in the afternoon, and I like the games we played last year in the evenings. I don't know why we have any lessons there at all. Even three in the morning seem three too many when you are by the seaside. Oh, by the way, I nearly forgot, here's a note Dr. Hende gave me for you this morning."

"I wonder what that's about," his mother said as she opened the envelope Peter had given her. ". . . 'should be obliged if you could come to see me at any convenient time in the near future' . . . Peter, have you been up to some mischief?"

Peter looked hurt. "No, Mother, really not. I've no idea what Dr. Hende wants to see you about."

"Would you tell him that I'll be coming to see him with you tomorrow morning after the main break at ten o'clock?"

"All right, Mother, I'll tell him when I get in at eight."

Punctually at ten the next morning, Peter and his mother knocked at the door marked "Teachers' Common Room". Dr. Hende was the only one there, as all the others had just gone to take their classes. He seemed a little embarrassed and not quite sure how to start. "Do come in, madam," he said, and cleared his throat nervously. "I have to discuss with you—ehem—something which is outside my own personal control. I mean to say—ehem—it's rather an awkward subject for me, but there it is . . ."

Peter's mother was getting more puzzled all the time. What on earth was Dr. Hende driving at? "Would you mind telling me why you have asked me to come here?" she demanded.

"Well, yes, as I was about to say, it's about our holiday camp at Henkendorf. Perhaps Peter would like to sit down over there while I tell you about it." He lowered his voice as he continued, "You see, there are bound to be some parents who will object to their sons living together for a fortnight with a Jewish boy. Not that this is anything against Peter or you, madam, of course. As you know, I have had the highest regard for you all for many years, but it isn't entirely up to me . . ."

"Dr. Hende, will you please come straight to the point? It's no concern of mine what other people think. Neither Peter nor his parents have done anything wrong, I gather, so what do you suggest we do?"

Dr. Hende fidgeted with his glasses. "Well, madam, it did just occur to me that it would make matters much easier all round if Peter could bring a medical certificate to say that it wasn't good for him at this stage to come to camp with us. This might prevent any—ehem—unpleasantness later, and Peter could just carry on in another class during the fortnight in question."

Peter's mother flushed with indignation. "Do you realize what you are suggesting?" she almost shouted at Dr. Hende. "My husband and I have brought Peter up all these years to become an upright and truthful citizen, and you, who are supposed to represent a nation which believes itself superior to us Jews—you suggest a mean dishonesty to save yourself difficulties. No, I'm afraid you'll have to find some other way out. If you or the Headmaster wish to bar Peter from going to camp that's your business, but if you do, he certainly won't bring a medical certificate, and he won't go into another class for that fortnight either."

She turned round and, leaving Dr. Hende standing in the middle of the room, took Peter by the arm, made straight for the door with him and stormed out.

By the time she had returned home, she wondered whether she had done the right thing.

"Do you think," she asked Peter's father, "it will harm you or Peter? After all, I shouted at a member of the National Socialist Party."

"I doubt it," Peter's father said, "but in any case, what's done is done; so we'll have to wait and see."

The very next day a letter came in the post. It was addressed to Peter's father, and read:

"Dear Sir,

For administrative reasons it will unfortunately not be possible for your son Peter to go to camp with his class this year. He is therefore excused from school while his class is away.

Heil Hitler!

A. WESTREICH.
Headmaster."

"All right, then," Peter's father said at dinner that day, "if they won't take you to the seaside, we will. We can just about manage one week. We can all do with a little holiday."

So, while Peter's form were on the train to Henkendorf, without Peter, Hans Golden and Paul Roth, Peter and his parents were busy packing a few things for their own trip to the seaside.

"Shall I order a taxi from the rank for tomorrow morning?" Peter asked. There was a rank just outside their front door and Peter knew most of the taxi-drivers.

"No," said his father, "I know we've always done that

when we've gone on holiday before, but let's save where we can now. We haven't much luggage, so we'll go by tram."

Carrying a case each, they arrived at the quayside, after a short tram ride, a few minutes before eight the next morning.

"I wonder which boat it'll be today," Peter said. Of the three boats which regularly made the seaside trip from Kolstatt, Peter liked the S.S. *Kolstatt* best. It was only three years old, and everything on board was still new and shiny. Moreover, it had twin propellers at the back, which enabled it to go faster and make bigger waves than the other two.

Peter could see two of the three boats moored at the quayside a little way from the tram stop. He recognized them by their yellow funnels with blue and white bands round them.

"Look, Mother, we're lucky," he called. "We'll be going by the *Kolstatt*."

"It beats me how on earth this boy always finds out this sort of thing," said his mother. "I wish he was as good at maths as he is at trams and boats!"

"But it's easy," Peter answered. "There's smoke coming out of the *Kolstatt's* funnel. That means they're getting her engines ready to go. The *Berlin* next to her is quite still, so she probably came back at ten last night. And I bet you we'll meet the *Heringsbeck* on the way."

"Brilliant, Sherlock Holmes," his father teased him. "Now watch that case as you go up the gangway."

"Let's go and sit at the back, please, Dad," Peter begged, as soon as they arrived on board. He had two favourite places on these boats: one was right at the bow, where he could peer over the top and watch the boat cut a path through the water and throw up a big white-capped wave. The other place was at the very back, where you could look down and watch the water being churned up as in a weir by the two big propellers. If you passed a smaller boat, you could watch it behind you dancing on the waves made by your boat. At the back you were sheltered, whilst at the bow it could be very windy when the boat was going fast. At the back there was also an enormous steering wheel. His Aunt Teresa had once explained to him that this was for use in case the proper one on the bridge broke down. He wasn't quite sure whether this was true or whether it was another of Aunt Teresa's leg-pulls, but in any case he loved sitting on the big box to which this wheel was attached.

He led the way there, greeting like long-lost friends two or three of the sailors he met, and settled himself on top of the box, next to the big steering wheel, with his father and mother occupying seats on the bench which surrounded it.

Punctually at eight o'clock, someone blew a whistle on the bridge, the gangway was lowered, and amid much shouting from the sailors working the winches and the dock-hands at the quayside, the ropes which had secured the boat to the side were undone from their bollards, dropped into the water and pulled on board. At the same time, the floor underneath Peter and his parents started vibrating.

"They've started up the engines," Peter called to his parents. "Look, we're moving!"

And so they were. Slowly the boat floated away from the side, and then, gathering speed, it started moving downstream. As it did so, Peter surveyed the view in front of him. He loved it all the better for having seen it many, many times: the quayside with the people, trams and cars growing smaller the further the boat moved away; behind it, where there had once been fortifications to defend the town, there was now a hill covered with grass and flowers, and at the top of it a skyline of public buildings well known for miles around.

Gradually this scene disappeared to give way to some mean and dingy dwelling houses, where some of Kolstatt's poor people lived. In another few minutes they had left the town proper and passed between factories and shipyards on both sides of the river. This had always been a dismal view, with hardly anyone working, but today Peter said to his father, "Look, Dad, it seems that some of those docks are going to open again. There's a lot of work going on everywhere. Are they going to build more boats for the seaside?"

"I wish they were," answered his father, "but from what people say it seems more likely that they'll build warships."

"But we learnt in History that Germany was forbidden to build warships when we lost the last war. Is that all changed again?"

"No," said his father, "it isn't, but our new government is secretly starting to get ready in case there should be another war."

"Why should anyone want to start another war?" Peter asked.

"I don't suppose they would," Peter's father answered, and then added in a low voice, "but I shouldn't wonder if Hitler wants to start another war when he's ready—only don't you ever say anything about that to anyone; that would be enough to get us all into the concentration camp."

"What are concentration camps, really, Dad?" Peter asked. "Everyone's talking about them, usually under their breath, but no one will really tell me anything."

"The less you know about those dreadful places, the better," Peter's father answered. "They are prison camps specially built by the Nazis for their enemies, and designed to make life as hellish as possible. People who are sent there never come out the same, if they come out at all. We don't really know many details, because the few who've returned have been so frightened that they've refused to talk about their experiences. Perhaps that's just as well. It saves us having nightmares. But what are we talking about all of a sudden? This is our holiday, so let's not worry about such things!"

Peter returned to his favourite occupation of watching the wake behind the boat and looking out at the landscape. He loved this part of the country better than any other. "Home" to Peter meant so many things: his parents' flat and his grandmother's; his school and the Buchwald; the country between Kolstatt and the sea, and miles and miles of wide beaches, golden with sand. And yet, he thought, I am only going on this trip today because some people in this country say this is not my home and I am not to go to camp with their children. If this isn't my home, what is? And what is the meaning of the word "home", if not the place where you have been brought up and have lived as long as you can remember?

As he sat there, lost in thought, the memory came back to him of snatches of conversation he had overheard at the lawyers' meeting in the spring: "At least send your children out of the country . . . Yes, but where . . .?"

Why, Peter thought, should I have to go away? What's the sense of it? Surely this is my home, I haven't any other. It doesn't make sense. I don't want to leave, I don't want to leave, I don't want . . .

"Look, Peter," his mother's voice interrupted his thoughts, "you can see Heringsbeck in the far distance already."

The trip had passed all too quickly for Peter. In what seemed no time at all the river had widened into a bay and they were in sight of the seaside resort of Heringsbeck, where they had spent many pleasant holidays, and where they were going to stay for the next week.

Peter watched the tiny row of houses by the Heringsbeck quay grow until you could see windows and doors; within minutes toy people by the quayside turned into real human beings, and soon the shouting and throwing of ropes between the boat and the pier was repeated in reverse. Up came the gangway, and with his case in one hand and his ticket in the other, Peter followed his parents off the boat.

The boarding house in which they usually stayed was on the sea-front, about fifteen minutes' walk from the pier. There were three ways of getting there if you had too much luggage for walking: first you could take a ramshackle old bus; second, there were ordinary taxis, like the ones in front of Peter's house at Kolstatt, and, third, there was Peter's favourite way, a horse-drawn cab.

Peter's luck was in, a cab was waiting, no one had booked it before Peter got off the boat, and his parents were willing to go in it. So he climbed up in front and sat on the seat next to the cabby. "Gee-up," the cabby called to his horse, and Peter from his high perch, watched the broad back of the horse below him slowly go into action and sway in time with the rhythmical "clop-trot, clop-trot" of its hooves on the cobbles. Looking down on the people of Heringsbeck, Peter was happy. He would willingly exchange all tram, bus and taxi rides for a cab ride, and perhaps even—but he wasn't quite so sure about that—the rides he sometimes had with Hans Golden and his family in their private car.

They were soon settled in the friendly little boarding house. The weather was hot and beautiful so that Peter could spend most of his time in the sea and digging elaborate earthworks in the sand. Just for a change every now and then he buried his father or his mother under piles of warm yellow sand until only their heads showed.

One evening as they were listening to the band which played near the pier, Peter suggested, "Let's go to Becker's Café afterwards, shall we? I feel just like eating one of their famous pastries."

"We really shouldn't spend too much money on extras this time," his mother answered. "Still, we used to go there almost every evening, so perhaps we can afford it just once."

Peter was delighted. Becker's was the best café in the town, and a favourite meeting place for holiday-makers. Peter was almost certain to meet someone he knew there; besides there was music, and Peter remembered the long talks he used to have with the pianist and the violinist during their interval.

They approached Becker's from the opposite side of the road, and Peter, who was the most observant member of the family, said, "Look, they've modernized the front, and repainted it all. Doesn't it look nice and new!"

When they reached the door, he went on, "And they've still got that funny little notice there saying 'Dogs not admitted'. There's another one underneath. Let's see what it says." He moved closer, because the second notice was covered by a shadow from a letter box. Suddenly the blood drained from his face. "Dad," he said—and he was full of a quiet fury that made his voice come out quite hoarse— "do you know what it says there? It says 'No Jews'. The very idea! Please let's go home at once."

He felt as if someone had given him a violent box on the ear, and then tied his hands behind his back so that he couldn't hit him back.

"I'm sorry, Peter," said his father, "but I'm afraid you'll

have to get used to this sort of thing. There are quite a few notices like these appearing all over the place. In some cases we've known that the people who put them up had always been Nazis. But sometimes we have unpleasant surprises like this one. Who would have thought that old Mr. Becker, who used to be so pleased to see us, and made such a fuss of you, Peter, when you were smaller—well," and Peter's father pulled himself up sharply—"I suppose we should have known that most of it was show. We're only now beginning to find out who our real friends are, and believe me, Peter, they're few and far between."

They had nearly reached their boarding house, when Peter's mother thought of something which she hoped would cheer Peter up a little. "I know what we'll do," she said. "Let's take a picnic lunch tomorrow and walk along the front to Zinnitz."

"Oh yes," Peter agreed excitedly, forgetting his disappointment. "That'll be lovely. I hope the weather stays nice."

Once again, Peter was lucky. He woke up to another sunny day, and they all set off along the beach with their picnic lunch. If you had asked Peter what he enjoyed most during his holiday, he would have answered without hesitation, "The boat trip there and the morning walk to Zinnitz." This was no ordinary walk. First they all took off their shoes and socks and started paddling along the water's edge. Then there were frequent halts to pick up shells and look for pieces of amber. From time to time they would sit and rest in the sand, put their shoes on again and go roaming through the dunes behind the beach, among the coarse grass and clusters of pine trees, only to return eventually to paddling. All this made for a good appetite, and they sat down to their picnic a mile before they reached Zinnitz.

"Let's just pop into Zinnitz for a bit," Peter's mother

said when they had finished. "I'd love to have a little look at their shops."

Peter didn't want to do this very much, but he had had it all his own way that morning and was quite prepared to make a concession now. So they all put their shoes and socks on once more and went over the dunes to the main road which led into the little town. They were still some way from the first houses, when Peter said, "Look, they've stretched a banner across the road. I wonder whether there's a fair on or something."

Alas, when they came a little closer, Peter had his second shock. The banner read:

"Jews! You'd best keep out of here.
We don't want you. Is that clear?"

CHAPTER 6

The Tram Ride

Gradually Peter began to grow a thick skin. It was no good upsetting yourself every time you saw something you didn't like. Now that he was looking out for them, he saw plenty of notices every day saying, "This is a German Undertaking", "This business is free from Jews" (as if Jews were some sort of infection!), or "Jews not allowed". He also saw plenty of headlines in the papers, which at one time would have upset him for the whole day. "World Jewry Blackens Germany's Name Abroad", for instance. What nonsense, he thought, and yet it gave him a feeling of uneasiness. He could never really enjoy anything for long these days before he was suddenly reminded that he and his people were not safe. He was always expecting some new unpleasantness round every corner, and it seemed to him that things were gradually becoming worse.

Perhaps it wasn't such a bad idea of his father's to try and send him to school abroad. He couldn't imagine himself in a foreign country, and yet he was beginning to think that it might be better there than at home so long as everyone here made it so clear that he and his people were not wanted.

Still, it wasn't in Peter's nature to be miserable for long at a time. Taken all in all he had thoroughly enjoyed his week at the seaside, and now that he was back, he still had another week's holiday at home before his form were due back from Henkendorf. He decided to do all the things he liked best in that time. He cleaned his desk out and tied up his souvenirs and his collected odds and ends. He spent a whole day writing out a catalogue of his books. One day Hans Golden asked him to go to the Buchwald with him and his parents in their car. Before long, there were only two days left.

"Dad, will you come swimming with me tomorrow, if it's fine?" he asked.

"I'm afraid I have some work out of town tomorrow," answered his father, and added, "thank goodness, because there isn't much work these days, as you know. But you go and have a swim by all means."

The next morning, Peter set out with his swim trunks rolled in his towel. He didn't take his bicycle. Since Rudi's death he hadn't been so keen on riding it. He and Rudi had usually cycled together, and it wasn't half as much fun on one's own. Perhaps it was really that he didn't want to be reminded too often that Rudi wasn't with him any more.

The first tram that came along had one of the open-sided summer trailers Peter liked, and he jumped on. Life wasn't so bad after all. He soon arrived at the lake with the swimming pool, and had a good time swimming and sunbathing.

The baths were half empty, since the school term hadn't
finished, and one or two of the attendants looked at him
as if they were sure he was playing truant. After a time
something inside him told Peter that dinner couldn't be far
away, so he collected his clothes, dressed and went back to
the tram stop.

This was the slack time of the day, and there was no
trailer. Although there were plenty of empty seats inside,
Peter occupied his favourite place right behind the driver on
the front platform. As they approached the inner suburbs,
the tram gradually filled up, but no one else joined Peter
on the platform. The tram turned a corner at the top of a
long hill, and as it started on its way down Peter could see
the whole centre of the town spread out below him. There
was the town hall with its odd turrets, the big old church with
its enormous yet elegant spire, the city museum, the theatre—
all the familiar landmarks were there, and behind them
flowed the River Koll from which the town had taken its
name.

At the bottom of the hill, Peter knew, the tram would
make a sharp turn to the left, and as it was going at its
slowest right on the bend, Peter would jump off if no cars
were coming. This would save him a minute on his short way
home from the tram stop, and he would be ready for his
dinner that minute sooner. Swimming always made him
hungry, and he started speculating what there might be for
dinner today . . .

All of a sudden he stopped thinking about his dinner.
What was going wrong? Trams often went down this hill at
a fair speed, but this one seemed to be going faster than
usual. They were nearly half-way down the hill now, and
the tram was rocking and lurching from side to side. Surely
the driver ought to be turning the big shiny brass handle

on his right: which applied the brake. A thought flashed through Peter's mind: Could this be a brake failure? But he realized at once that it had nothing to do with that. The driver hadn't even touched the brake handle. Peter glanced briefly over his shoulder, and through the glass panel behind him he saw that some of the passengers were looking worried. Before he could turn round again, he heard a thud and something fell against his legs. He looked down and found that the driver had collapsed at his feet.

Peter's first impulse was to pull on the bell like mad and summon the conductor. But, no, that would take too long. He could see the sharp bend at the bottom, and he knew that the tram must be stopped at once if it wasn't to jump the rails and run straight into Schmidt's Department Store. Without a moment's hesitation, Peter grabbed at the brake handle with both hands and turned with all his might. Goodness, how hard it was to move, and yet it had seemed so easy when he had watched the drivers do it! The bend was racing nearer, and the tram was still lurching like one possessed, trying to shake Peter off. He pressed himself against the controls, strained every muscle in his body, and kept on turning the brake handle. It's no good, he thought, I'd better jump off this platform before we get to the bottom. At least I'll only have a couple of broken legs then . . . No, I cannot do that, I must stop this tram, I must, I MUST . . . and just then he heard a sound which started as a whistle but quickly grew into a metallic scream and clatter. He had never heard a more welcome noise in all his life, for this was the sound the brakes made when they gripped the wheels. It seemed an eternity, but it was probably only two or three seconds until the tram reached the curve, still at a good speed. Peter's head was filled by only one thought: Will we make it, will we make it, will we make it?

The next thing he knew, he was picking himself off the floor of the platform and hearing a lot of agitated voices coming nearer. The tram had stopped now, but had jolted so much when it shot round the bend that it had sent Peter flying. The door between the platform and the inside of the carriage was wrenched open, and a white-faced conductor came tottering through it, followed by those of the passengers who had recovered sufficiently to stand on their own legs again.

"Heaven help us!" the conductor said. "Whatever's the matter with my mate?"

Peter had forgotten about the driver in his excitement, and as he and the conductor both bent over him, the man opened his eyes and said weakly, "What happened? Did I pass out?"

"Yes, you did," said Peter, "just half-way down the hill."

"But how did the tram stop?" the conductor wanted to know.

"I stopped it," said Peter, "and please, can I sit down a minute?"

Things had happened much too quickly for Peter to think about anything except what he had had to do. Now, all of a sudden, he realized what a terrible danger he and the other passengers had just lived through, and the mere thought of it made him feel quite weak in the knees. He sat down on the nearest seat, and was instantly surrounded by a little crowd of passengers and passers-by.

"Get him some water, he's going to faint," he heard someone say.

"Yes, and a glass for the driver too, he's been taken ill," someone else said.

"What's the boy done?" inquired another voice.

"He stopped the tram from crashing when the driver fainted," came the reply. "Saved all our lives, I reckon."

Someone came out of the department store opposite and handed a glass of lemonade to Peter and one to the driver, who was now sitting opposite Peter inside the tram. Peter drank his lemonade and felt his strength coming back. He rose from his seat, thanked the lady who had brought his drink, and was just going to get off, when an Inspector appeared on the scene.

"Hello, young man!" he said. "I hear that you've just shown great presence of mind and very bravely stopped this runaway tram. What's your name?"

"Peter Cronheim."

"Right, Peter," the Inspector continued. "If you'll please take me to your parents, we'll tell them what happened and then we can write a full report of the incident. I have an idea that the Transport Department and the Mayor will be very pleased with you, young man."

Peter's mother opened the door when they arrived at the flat and she looked startled when she saw the Inspector.

"Good morning, Inspector," she said. "Has my boy been up to something?"

"On the contrary, madam," answered the Inspector. "I have to congratulate you on having a son who is a credit to you and to all of us in Kolstatt. If you'll kindly allow me to come in, I should like to tell you how your Peter has just saved a number of lives. Perhaps you wouldn't mind if I write my report in here?"

"Why, certainly, Inspector," Peter's mother answered. "I'd no idea, please tell me quickly."

They went into the sitting-room, and during the next half hour they somehow managed to put on paper a reasonable account of what had happened on the tram.

Peter had forgotten all about his appetite and in the general excitement his mother forgot all about her dinner until she was reminded of it by a smell of burning.

"Good gracious, Inspector, please excuse me," she cried, as she darted towards the kitchen. "I clean forgot that I had left the gravy on the stove!"

"Never mind, madam," said the Inspector when Peter's mother came back from the kitchen a moment later. "Burnt gravy is nothing compared to the broken bones we might

have had to deal with. You've cause to be exceedingly grateful to Providence—and to your son—today. I must go now,
but I'm sure you'll hear from the Transport Department very
soon. Good afternoon, madam, and good afternoon, Peter.
Carry on as you are, my lad, and you'll go a long way."

Peter's appetite had come back with a vengeance and he
and his mother sat down to dinner as soon as the Inspector
had left. Peter was just finishing his second helping of pan-
cakes with jam, when the door bell rang. Peter pushed the
last piece into his mouth, jumped up and ran to the door,
followed more slowly by his mother.

There was a stranger outside.

"Excuse me, but you are Peter Cronheim, aren't you?"

"Yes," said Peter, rather pleased at being wanted, "but
who are you?"

"I'm from the *Kolstatt Daily Journal*," said the stranger.
"I wonder if you would mind telling me exactly what happened on the tram this morning?"

"Why, is it going to be printed in the papers?" Peter asked
eagerly.

"Of course it is," answered the reporter. "I should like
to have the story straight from you, to make sure we get it
right."

"Ask the gentleman to come inside, Peter," his mother
said quietly. At this moment it would have been hard to tell
which one was the proudest, mother or son.

Peter was in his element. This was only the second time
in his life that he had made any impression on the adult
world. The first had been when he had helped with the
election, and afterwards he had felt that his efforts hadn't
been very successful. There was no such doubt in his mind
now. He suddenly realized that the whole of Kolstatt would
be reading about him in the paper tomorrow, and decided

that if every detail wasn't correct, it wasn't going to be his fault.

As he was still on holiday the next day, he could have stayed in bed until his mother called him. But he was far too excited. When he heard someone at the front door about half-past six, he jumped out of bed to see if it was the newspaper. But no—it was only the baker's boy. Peter went back to bed with his eyes wide open and ears straining to hear any little sound outside.

After a very long quarter of an hour the letter box rattled, and before it had even stopped moving Peter was there. He tore the paper open, and there it was—in the headlines:

LOCAL BOY HERO SAVES 17 LIVES
STOPS TRAM JUST IN TIME

Underneath this Peter read his whole story—or nearly all of it. One or two details were missing, and among them, strangely, was his name. He hardly noticed this at the time, because he was too busy reading it all and looking at the photograph of the tram standing where he had stopped it.

A short while later the postman came, and, as expected, brought a letter from the Transport Department addressed to Peter's father. Peter ran in to his father's bedroom with it and asked him to open it. This is what it said:

"Dear Sir,

It has been brought to my notice that your son Peter yesterday averted what would undoubtedly have been a major traffic disaster through commendable presence of mind and without regard to his own safety. After consultation with the Mayor, I have decided that our thanks should be expressed to your son at a small public ceremony. I should be glad therefore if you would kindly permit him to come to the Mayor's office in the Town Hall tomorrow, Sunday, at 3 p.m. Members of the boy's immediate family will be welcome.

Heil Hitler!

(Signed) OBELSAMMEL.
Director
Transport Department."

For Peter that Saturday and Sunday morning couldn't go quickly enough. He was fidgety, he couldn't concentrate, he did everything in a hurry, as if someone was chasing him. All the time he was thinking of "the ceremony". He wondered what it would be like. What were all these important people going to say to him or about him? And would he have to reply in public? He very much hoped not, for he had never spoken before an audience, and was really rather frightened of it. There would probably be Press photographers to take his picture together with the Mayor and the Director of the Transport Department, and probably reporters as well who would write another article for the papers. He wondered how many people would be invited: fifty? a hundred? or even more?

Peter's mother and father decided to go with him, and so did his Oma, Aunt Teresa and Aunt Lucie. Only Uncle Martin and Aunt Katie said they wouldn't go, although of course they were very proud of Peter. Uncle Martin said he didn't think at a time like this Jews ought to make themselves conspicuous in any way.

Peter also found a pretext to knock at the door of Mr. Schulz, the lodger, and no sooner had he delivered his message than he started proudly to tell the whole tram episode all over again. Peter was a little surprised to find that Mr. Schulz hadn't heard anything about it because he

thought that everyone in the tram section of the Kolstatt Transport Department should have known about it by now. Mr. Schulz made some excuse about not having been to work that Friday and Saturday as he had had some business of his own to see to, and he made up for his ignorance by appearing most interested and pleased with Peter's exploit.

"So when did you say the ceremony will be?" he asked.

"Tomorrow afternoon at three o'clock," Peter answered.

"And will your parents go with you?" Mr. Schulz wanted to know.

"Yes, they certainly will," Peter said, "and my Oma and my two aunts."

"Will they really?" said Mr. Schulz, evidently pleased about something, although Peter couldn't imagine why this particular piece of information should have pleased him so much.

At last Sunday dinner, eaten a little earlier than usual, was over. Although the Town Hall was only ten minutes' walk away, overlooking the River Koll, Peter's father thought they might as well travel in style on this occasion. They took a taxi from the rank outside their house, collected Oma and the two aunts, and arrived at the Town Hall with a quarter of an hour to spare.

Peter's father introduced himself to the commissionaire at the door.

"I'm Mr. Cronheim. We have come to attend a ceremony at the Mayor's office."

"Oh yes, I know, sir," the commissionaire beamed. "Let me see now, this must be your son. I read all about you in the paper, young man. Well done, well done. We need more like you. As a matter of fact one of my neighbours says she was just coming out of Schmidt's Department Store when she saw this here tram hurtling down the hill like a bomb. She wondered what the matter was, but she never guessed there was a schoolboy stopping it."

Peter blushed with pride. He was getting so well known that soon, he thought, people would be stopping him in the street.

"If you will please go up this main staircase to the first floor with your son, Mr. Cronheim," the commissionaire continued, "you'll see the Mayor's ante-room on your right. The Mayor will be there in a minute. And if the other members of the family will please go on to the Conference Chamber on the second floor, they can wait there for the ceremony."

CHAPTER 7

The Search

Peter flew up the stairs to the first floor two steps at a time, followed more decorously by his father. His other relations had two flights to climb, so they started off even more slowly.

"Come on, Dad," Peter called out impatiently from the top of the stairs. "We mustn't keep the Mayor waiting."

"All right, Peter," his father answered, "there's plenty of time. It's only ten minutes to three."

They stepped into the Mayor's ante-room and sat down on two comfortable plush-covered chairs. Peter had never seen the Mayor, but he knew from his lessons that he was a full-time civil servant paid by the government. He had seen pictures of him in the paper, and he spent the next few minutes imagining what the Mayor was going to say to him, and what he would answer. He was so busy day-dreaming that he didn't notice the time go by.

"I say, the Mayor is late," said his father, looking at his pocket watch. "It's five past three already."

After a few more minutes, the door from the Mayor's office opened, and the Mayor came in. Peter looked at him in surprise. This wasn't the same smiling, happy man he had seen in the papers from time to time. He looked old, tired, and worried. Whatever is the matter? Peter thought. Surely on an occasion like this he should be happy?

"You are Mr. Cronheim, I take it," he said to Peter's father without a smile, "and this is your brave son Peter, is it?"

He shook them both by the hand, and then continued, "I am personally delighted to meet you, and especially this promising young man. That makes it all the more awkward for me to say what I have to say because I know it will be most upsetting for you both."

He paused, obviously embarrassed, and Peter looked at him anxiously. He wondered what was coming next.

"I am afraid I received a telephone call a few minutes ago from the National Socialist Party Headquarters. They informed me that on no account will they allow a public ceremony in honour of a Jew no matter how deserving he may be. I cannot tell you how unhappy I am about this, and I can assure you I have grown old and grey in the last few months with all the interference I've had to put up with. But I am afraid there is nothing I can do about it, absolutely nothing."

"I quite understand, Mr. Mayor," Peter's father said sharply. "I should have known better than to allow Peter to come here today."

"But, Dad"—Peter was not too distressed to stick up for his father—"it isn't your fault! If the Nazis don't want us, we'll go somewhere else." His pride was dreadfully hurt, but he wouldn't let the Mayor notice for anything in the world.

"What a high-principled boy," the Mayor said. "It's a shame. He would make such a good German, if only they'd let him be one."

"Maybe I don't want to be a German," Peter snapped, against his better judgement; but he was determined to appear as if he didn't mind.

The Mayor pretended that he hadn't heard Peter's remark, and went on, "Of course we shall send on his reward and a letter of commendation. There can be no objection to that."

"Thank you, Mr. Mayor," Peter's father said, "and good-bye."

"Heil Hit . . . I am sorry, good-bye, Mr. Cronheim, good-bye, Peter."

As they walked home, Peter said to his father, "I don't think I want to stay in this country any longer than I have to."

"But you don't know what it's like anywhere else," his father said. He was surprised at Peter's sudden change of mind.

"No, but I'd rather be less comfortable than be treated as if I had some disease or was a second-rate person."

"Well," said his father, "since you've come to feel this way now, I may as well tell you that we have had an offer from a school in Belgium which would accept you. The only problem is to get the money to pay for your fees over there, since the Nazis will not allow us to send German money abroad. Still, where there's a will there's a way. I suppose we'll manage something. But it'll be a hard wrench for your mother to let you go abroad."

"It won't be easy for me either, Dad," Peter said. "One half of me wants very much to stay at home, but every now and then I get into such a temper about the Nazis that I feel I should really like to pick up my things on the spot and leave. All the same, I wish you and Mother could come too."

"I don't know if your mother and I aren't better off staying here," his father said. "You see, we're not so young any more, and it would be very hard for us to start from the beginning again somewhere else, where we might not even be able to speak the language. Nothing lasts for ever, and I don't suppose the Nazis will."

Peter and his father arrived at the flat before Peter's mother, who had gone home with his Oma and aunts first.

"That's odd," said Peter's father, as he tried to turn the key in the front door. "I could have sworn I locked the door when we left, and yet it's not locked now." He pushed the door open and switched on the light in the hall.

"Oh Dad!" Peter shouted. "We've had burglars!"

Everything was in disorder. The coats that had been hanging on the hooks were now lying higgledy-piggledy on the floor with their pockets turned inside out.

They pushed open the door to the sitting-room and found books strewn all over the tables and floor. Strangely, the dining-room, where they kept the family silver, had hardly been touched. Before he went to his own room, Peter looked at his father. He wasn't red in the face as he usually was when he was angry; he had gone quite pale and quiet.

"What's the matter, Dad?" Peter asked. "It's a nuisance, having burglars, but we're insured, aren't we?"

"This is no burglary," Peter's father answered. "Nothing valuable seems to have been stolen. No, Peter, our flat has been searched."

"Whatever for, Dad?" Peter wanted to know. "You're not a spy, or in politics, or anything."

"I wish I knew what they expected to find here. At least I could explain to them that I haven't got it. I've kept out of politics completely, apart from going to elections, because I didn't want us to become labelled 'enemies of the National Socialist State'. But it looks as if the Nazis are suspecting me of something all the same."

Peter ran into his room. He pushed the door open—and his heart sank. Nothing had been touched except the one thing he cared about: his desk had been completely rifled. All the books he had so carefully sorted only a couple of days earlier were scattered over his settee. The drawers had been taken from the desk and stacked on the floor. His drawings had evidently been examined and put back in disorder on the desk. The folder in which he kept the few letters that his friends and relatives had written to him was missing altogether. And, worst of all, his favourite little glass dog lay broken on the floor. Someone must have trodden on it. Only his three monkeys were still standing in their old place, and it seemed to Peter that now they were mocking him with their advice to "see no evil, hear no evil and speak no evil".

"Dad," Peter called to his father, who was going through the mess in the sitting-room, "I cannot find the folder with my letters anywhere."

"I don't suppose you will, Peter," his father called back. "They've taken all my letters as well."

"Whatever for?" Peter asked.

"I suppose they'll try very hard to find something in them

which they can say was 'anti-German' so that they can justify their search. Actually, they won't find a thing, because I've always been most careful. But what worries me is that they've taken my address book away as well. Now I cannot write to anyone whose address I don't happen to remember, and I'm afraid that includes my friend who sent us the list of schools in Belgium and the one that offered to take you."

"What use is your address book to them, Dad?" Peter asked.

"I expect they'd like to find someone in there who is on their black list, and then they can say I was a friend of a communist or something like that."

"And were you?" Peter asked anxiously.

"Of course not," Peter's father answered, and in spite of the grim situation they were in he couldn't help smiling at Peter's concern.

"I wonder what Mr. Schulz will say, when he . . . ouch!" Peter cried out, as he tripped over something on the floor of the hall.

"What's the matter?" his father asked, looking out of the sitting-room door.

"I nearly fell over something here," Peter said. "Whatever is it?"

Peter picked up a small round metal object, partly encased in rubber and at the end of a wire lead.

"Well, I'll be damned!" His father fairly shouted the words and it startled Peter because his father was usually so quiet. "It's a microphone! Now I see it all. It's that fellow Schulz. Do you remember when he told your mother he was a radio enthusiast and asked to lay his aerial on the hall floor? Well, that was it: a secret microphone to spy on us in case we said anything against the German state or the Nazis. Since he couldn't catch us out on anything, he asked his

fellows from the Secret Police to come and have a look round. Let's go to his room. I'm willing to wager that he's packed up and gone."

Peter's father was right. Mr. Schulz's room was perfectly tidy and untouched. All his things were gone, and so, of course, was he.

They hadn't got very far with their tidying when the door bell rang. They both went out to open the door, half expecting to find a policeman, but unwilling to admit this to each other. Outside the door were Peter's mother and Mrs. Laumann, a non-Jewish lady who lived with her husband and son on the third floor.

Before Peter or his father could explain anything, Peter's

mother said, "Hello, I hope you're not too disappointed, Peter. The Mayor told us that there couldn't be a ceremony after all. You know Mr. Laumann works in the office next to the Mayor's, and Mrs. Laumann heard all about you from him. So she came along to see you, but as it's all off, I've brought her here for coffee."

Peter's father tried to tell them both what had happened while they had been out. But he couldn't get a word in before Mrs. Laumann grasped Peter's hand and shook it hard.

"I'm delighted to be able to shake hands with you," she said, beaming. "I think you are a splendid young man and I'm terribly proud to live in the same house with you. I couldn't care less about the Nazis, and I hope you don't, even though my husband has to be careful in his job as a civil servant . . ."

"Please, Mrs. Laumann," Peter's father interrupted at last, "will you come in and lower your voice, I am afraid I have some unpleasant things to tell my wife and you, but walls have ears nowadays, and we don't all want to get into trouble."

He shut the front door behind the two ladies and led them into the sitting-room. There he told them as quickly as he could the whole sad story of the search.

"Well I never!" said Mrs. Laumann when he had finished. "I often wondered how low some of my fellow-Germans could sink. This really takes the biscuit! Will you please do me the favour of coming to my flat for coffee this afternoon, and then we'll all come down afterwards and finish clearing up this dreadful mess?"

"That is very kind of you, Mrs. Laumann," said Peter's father. "But really I'm not sure whether it is altogether wise. By harbouring and helping us, you might endanger your husband's job and your son's future. You know the Nazis don't like people who are friendly with Jews, and . . ."

"Poppycock!" Mrs. Laumann cut him short. "What do I care about the Nazis? I'm as good a German as any of them, in fact a lot better, I think. If they want something from me, let them come and tell me. I'll see to it that my husband doesn't lose his job—I won't shout loudly enough for that, and besides my son is in the Nazi youth movement, so what do they want from me? I know he only joined because he had to, but they don't know that. Come along upstairs now, and we'll have some coffee."

With a wide gesture of the arm she swept them all out of the room and shepherded them upstairs to her third-floor flat.

Her husband greeted them politely and warmly, and listened sympathetically to the story of their last mishap. Every now and then he shook his head sadly and muttered, "I don't know what we are coming to. I don't know where it will all end." When they had finished, he said, "I'm glad my son is out today. I don't know how I could have faced him this afternoon, knowing that my fellow Germans are so beastly to our Jewish friends and neighbours. Well, let's do what we can to make up for it, and help you straighten your place out again."

They all trooped downstairs, and before long had the Cronheim flat looking tidy again. Peter was the last to finish, for he wouldn't allow anyone to help him. After all, only he knew the exact place for every one of his belongings. He even swept up the remains of his glass dog very carefully. He couldn't bear to throw them away and, making sure that no one was looking, he put all the bits into an old envelope, and hid it away in one of the drawers of his desk.

It was supper time when he had finished. Tomorrow he

would go back to school to meet his friends who had been to Henkendorf. They probably hadn't even heard yet of his exploit on the tram. Well, after today, he wasn't going to be the first one to tell them. Let them find out for themselves.

CHAPTER 8

Peter to the Rescue

It wasn't easy for Peter to settle down to the ordinary school routine again. So much had happened to him that didn't affect his classmates. His father had almost no work and the family was worried about money. His best friend had died. He had narrowly missed being made a hero in his home town, only to be reminded that as a Jew he was not wanted in Germany. Now even the Secret Police were interested in him and his family.

Most of the boys in his class were happy in the belief that Germany was going from strength to strength and that theirs was a glorious future. Peter, on the other hand, was faced by what seemed like a blank wall, barely tolerated where he was, and yet unable to see where else he could go. He became more

friendly with Hans Golden and Paul Roth, his two fellow-
Jews in class, although he didn't really like them and was
always comparing them with Rudi who had been so much
nicer. Of the non-Jews, only Walter Abel didn't seem to mind
speaking to him and Peter and Walter became quite friendly.

After morning break one day in the next week, Peter was
revising the words his class was supposed to learn for Latin.
The usual pandemonium raged round him as it always did
just before one of Mr. Senner's Latin periods. Soon the door
opened, and, to Peter's surprise, an immediate hush fell upon
the class. He looked up startled—there was never a hush
when Mr. Senner came in—and he found himself looking
straight at Dr. Westreich, the Headmaster.

Peter had heard his father say that once upon a time
Dr. Westreich had been a staunch German Democrat, but as
soon as the Nazis had come to power he had realized that his
bread was now buttered on the other side and had become,
if not an over-enthusiastic, at least a good Nazi. Peter could
no longer respect him, but of course he still had to do as he
was told. After all, a Headmaster was a Headmaster.

"Heil Hitler!" Dr. Westreich saluted the boys who were
all standing up quietly and wondering why the Headmaster
had come in place of Mr. Senner.

"Heil Hitler!" the class answered.

"Sit down, boys," continued the Headmaster. "You will
wonder why I am here this morning, so I will come straight to
the point. You all know that Mr. Senner had much good to
offer us. But there was one side to him which I am afraid we
could no longer ignore. He did not recognize the fact that
the National Socialist Party has at last rescued Germany
from a fate worse than death. He openly said that he would
not help the Party in any way. We tried to convince him of
the greatness of our new Germany, but he did not even com-

"We must morally click our heels. . . ."

promise by keeping quiet and watching our glorious new government get under way. So he left us no alternative but to let the authorities know of his attitude. He was arrested last night and will be brought before a proper law court as soon as possible. I wanted to tell you all this so that you should hear what really happened rather than listen to all sorts of rumours which will no doubt become current. I think you will all agree with me that we must morally click our heels before a government which has the strength of its convictions, and we can only hope that Mr. Senner, after he has received his due punishment, may see the error of his ways. Heil Hitler!"

Dr. Westreich turned smartly and marched out of the room, while the boys all rose from their desks and returned his Hitler salute. Peter was too stunned by this news to look around, but had he done so he would have noticed that most of the other boys were quite unconcerned. Only Walter Abel, who now occupied the seat next to Peter, looked worried. As soon as the Headmaster had left the room, Walter whispered to Peter, "You know what that means, don't you?"

"No, what?" Peter replied.

"It's the concentration camp. My father said that's where the Nazis put all those who disagree with their politics."

"How terrible," Peter said. "He was such a friendly man, and . . ."

"Who d'you think is going to take us for Latin now, Peter?" Paul Roth called across from the next row.

"Is that all you care about?" Peter snapped back. "How do I know?"

This started a general guessing game, which only stopped when Dr. Hende entered a few minutes later and introduced himself as their new Latin master.

The next morning was Midsummer's Day, and the sun was

warm and bright. When Dr. Hende called out the class register for absentees, all the boys were there except Hans Golden. That's odd, Peter thought. He wouldn't be likely to have a cold at this time of the year. Why should he be absent? Suddenly he remembered the morning when Rudi had been missing from school. It seemed hours of waiting until lunch time when at last he could go home.

The minute he was inside the door he said to his mother, "Hans Golden was missing from school today. Do you know if anything is wrong?"

His mother hesitated. "Well, not wrong exactly," she said after an uncomfortable pause. "Your father told me this morning in strict confidence that the Goldens wanted to try to run away and go abroad, as they didn't think there was any future for them in Germany."

"Then why didn't they leave in the ordinary way, instead of 'running away', as you say?" Peter asked.

"For two reasons," his mother answered. "The Nazis can be very difficult about letting grown-ups leave the country. In fact sometimes they lock them up instead. And secondly, if they do allow any Jews to leave, they don't let them take any of their belongings or money with them."

"But how are the Goldens going to live abroad without money?" Peter asked again.

"I don't know, but I imagine Hans's father has friends abroad and has somehow managed to let them have some of his money. Also, he's a very resourceful and enterprising man who will do well by his own efforts wherever he goes. He was the only one in our circle of friends who had a car, as you know, and he always made enough money to live comfortably."

"Don't you think we might all get out together by running away one day too?" Peter asked.

"I don't think so," said his mother wistfully. "However much we might like to, we've neither the means nor the know-how. We shall consider ourselves very lucky if we manage to send you to school abroad."

"Really, Peter, wake up! How long have I got to shake you?"

Peter slowly became conscious of another day. Yes, that's right, yesterday the Goldens had run away, so now he would have to go to school and find another friend missing from his class.

He opened his eyes. His mother stood over him, fully dressed. This surprised him. Usually she was in her dressing-gown when she called him. He looked at her more searchingly, and in spite of his sleepiness, he noticed that her eyes were very red, as if she had been crying.

"Is anything the matter, Mother?" he asked.

"Yes, very much, I'm afraid," she answered, and her voice quivered. "Two men from the Secret Police came at three this morning and took your father away with them."

"Oh!" Peter cried. A great lump came into his throat and choked him. "It could mean the concentration camp. We must get him back! What can we do?"

"Darling, if I knew that I should be the happiest woman on earth."

A numbing terror came over Peter. He had heard the dreadful stories about concentration camps and he was so afraid of losing his father into one of them that he could think of nothing else. Automatically, like a machine, he dressed and ate a little breakfast.

"I can't go to school, Mother," he said when he had finished. "I can't think of anything but Dad. Why should they want him? He hasn't done anything, has he?"

"Of course not," said his mother, "but they may think he has, or they may even pin something on him. Ever since they searched our house I've been worried. I only wish I knew where he was . . ." and she burst into tears.

Peter put a protective arm round her. "Well, that settles it. I'll go and try to find Dad for you. If you go, they might keep you as well. But I shouldn't be any good to them, so I'll go."

Peter had made up his mind, and whatever his mother said fell on deaf ears. He put on his school cap and said, "Wish me luck, Mother, and don't fret. I'll let you know every now and then how I'm doing."

And with that he ran downstairs.

It was only when Peter arrived in the street that he realized how hopelessly unprepared he was for the task he had set himself. He didn't even know where he should go to ask about his father. He stopped in front of his door, wondering which way to turn.

I'll ask at the Police Station, he thought. They are bound to know. He hadn't had much to do with the police in his life. Policemen were rather remote figures, wearing blue uniforms and shiny black helmets, usually controlling the traffic during processions and marches or at busy cross-roads. The only policeman who had ever been more to him than a figure in a uniform was a young man who, many years ago, used to call for their maid on her afternoon off. He would wait outside their door, and the way he hugged his helmet under his left arm had always looked to Peter as if he was carrying a spare head.

He had been to a Police Station only once in his life. This was three years ago when he had found a purse lying in the road. He had taken it straight to the Station, where a benevolent old policeman with a bald head and a walrus moustache had taken charge of it and then given him a lecture about the long term benefits of honesty.

Having decided where to go, Peter walked briskly down the road. As he turned into the street where his local Police Station was, he thought about the strange contrast between his last call there and his present mission. On the first occasion he had handed in a purse, and this time he was going to ask to be given back his father. He wondered how he would be received. He had heard that some policemen were quite good-natured, but he knew that others were grumpy and disagreeable, and that some of the younger ones were very keen Nazis. He felt just as he had done that Sunday afternoon last autumn when he had helped with the election: a little bit afraid, but conscious of having to do something really important.

He opened the door of the Police Station and stepped from the bright light of the summer morning into a small dim hall. When his eyes had accustomed themselves to the darkness, he looked around and saw a notice on one of the doors in front of him which read "Inquiries". This is it, he thought to himself, summoned his courage, and tried to look as unconcerned as he could. Then he pushed open the door.

He entered a small room with a window at the far end. Right across the width of the room ran a counter which divided it into half. On Peter's side of the counter the room was completely bare, except for a great many notices in small gothic print on a large notice board. On the far side of the room under the window were two desks. At each of them sat a policeman. One was sorting through a pile of cards and the other was writing with a scratchy pen on a big piece of paper. Neither of them took the slightest notice of Peter.

Funny, Peter thought, without their helmets they look almost like ordinary clerks in an office. For a few moments he stood quietly waiting. He didn't want to irritate them by making any move before one of them was ready to speak to him. Perhaps they didn't hear me come in, he thought, and gave a little cough. That worked. Without looking up, one of the policemen said to the other, "Your turn," and went on with his work.

The second policeman then turned his head slowly towards Peter, rose from his chair and ambled over to the counter. With the bright light from the window straight behind the man, Peter couldn't see his face very well, but he seemed to be young. I hope it isn't one of those young Nazis, he

thought. He was just about to make some stammering intro-
duction, when the policeman spoke:

"Hello, I know you, don't I? Aren't you Peter Cronheim?"

Peter turned pale. Was he as well known to the police as
his father was? He wanted to turn about and run straight
out of the building. No, he couldn't do that, because then
he was sure to be arrested and questioned. He had to stand
his ground.

The policeman didn't seem to notice Peter's fright and
continued: "You've grown since I saw you last. I used to
call at your flat sometimes when Christine worked for your
parents. Remember her? She's my wife now."

You could have knocked Peter down with a feather. What
a lucky chance! Of all the policemen in Kolstatt he had met
the only one he knew. He was so relieved that he almost
forgot for the moment the terrible worry that had brought
him to the Police Station.

"Yes, of course I remember Christine," Peter said. "How
is she?"

"Oh, well enough, thank you. We often talk about you all.
She'll be very pleased when I tell her I've spoken to you. Is
there anything I can do for you?"

"Well," Peter said, "I should like to know . . ." He
hesitated, not quite sure how to start the subject. "I mean,
could you perhaps help me to find . . ." He stopped again,
felt himself blush, and had to clear his throat. He was afraid
to say what he knew he had to, in case his only friend in the
police force said "No". If that happened, Peter believed that
his only chance to find his father would be lost. He wanted
to postpone the awful moment as long as possible.

"Well?" the policeman asked.

Peter knew it was now or never.

"Please, my father was arrested in the night. I want to find him."

Well, it was out, at any rate. Peter peered anxiously into the policeman's face to find out how he would react to this news.

"Oh," the policeman said, and he suddenly looked serious. "I'm sorry about that." He looked over his shoulder to see whether his colleague had been listening to their conversation. But he turned back again reassured: the scratching noises from the other man's pen continued uninterrupted.

"Do you know if your father had done anything wrong for which he might be wanted?"

"I'm quite sure he hasn't," Peter answered, and then he added urgently, "Please, can you help me find him and get him back?"

"Well, Peter," the policeman answered, "this won't be easy. You see, we don't deal with anything like that here. I'll try and find out something for you if I can, but I have to be careful. I have my job to keep. If I find out anything, I'll ask Christine to call on your mother. I'd better not be seen going to a Jewish flat myself."

"Thank you ever so much," Peter said. "Do you think there's anything else I can do?"

"You could try the Central Police Headquarters by the river," the policeman answered. "If you promise not to mention my name, I can tell you someone who may have some information."

"Certainly I won't mention your name," Peter said eagerly.

"Just ask for Sergeant Scheck. There's a chance that he may know something, but don't be disappointed if he doesn't."

"Thank you so very much," Peter said, and before the

policeman could wish him luck, he had dashed outside into the street again and was on his way down towards the River Koll.

The Central Police Headquarters was a big grey building, looking solid and forbidding. At the side it had some windows which were small and heavily barred. These belonged to the cells where people were kept until they went to a proper prison. Peter had always taken this place for granted. He had passed it hundreds of times but it had never occurred to him that he or any of his family would ever have anything to do with it. They had always been law-abiding citizens, and the Police Headquarters were for people who had fallen foul of the law.

Now he would have to go right inside this unknown place. As he walked up to it he felt his heart beating. Would they let him see this Sergeant Scheck? And if they did, what sort of a man was he? Surely he couldn't be as lucky again as he had been at his local Police Station.

The large wooden entrance door felt heavy. With an effort Peter pushed it open and stepped inside. He found himself in a large, cool, stone hall. In front of him was a wide staircase, which reminded him of something he couldn't quite remember. Of course, he thought after a moment, it's like the one in the Town Hall. It was less than a fortnight since he had stood proudly at the bottom of that other staircase. Still, it was no good standing there thinking about the past when something had to be done at once.

He looked around and saw a notice which said in large letters:

NO ADMITTANCE EXCEPT ON BUSINESS

"And what do you think you're doing in here, sonny? Sightseeing?" a shrill voice said behind him.

Peter jumped with fright and turned round. He hadn't noticed the little window marked "Information" just inside the door. Now an unpleasant looking middle-aged policeman was hanging out of it with a leer on his face, which suggested to Peter that his chances here were not too good.

"P-please," he stuttered in his confusion, "I have to see Sergeant Scheck."

"Well, fancy that!" the policeman said. "Fancy *having* to see Sergeant Scheck! No one *has* to see anyone here. Do you know what I'm here for? I am here to decide who may come in and see anyone. See that notice there? We're much too busy to allow every Tom, Dick and Harry to come and waste our time. What d'you want to see Sergeant Scheck for?"

Peter had to think quickly. He nearly said that the policeman at his local station had sent him here, but he remembered just in time that he had promised not to mention him. Suddenly an idea came to him.

"I'm the boy who stopped the tram from crashing a little while back, and I just wondered if I might . . ."

The policeman's face changed from a leer to a hideous grin as he interrupted Peter, "Well, for goodness' sake, why didn't you say so before? Of course you may see Sergeant Scheck. Just sit on that bench over there while I let him know on the telephone that you are here."

Peter sat down, rather pleased that his little ruse had worked so well. So far, so good, he thought. I wonder what Sergeant Scheck will be like.

A few moments later he heard the clanking of a heavy pair of boots down the stone staircase. He looked up and saw a burly policeman with a round red face and a double chin. Peter stood up and walked towards him. "Sergeant Scheck?" he inquired.

"That's me, young man," the Sergeant beamed. "I hear you are the chap who stopped the runaway tram. Well done, well done. What can I do for you now?"

"Well, Sergeant," Peter said, "I haven't really come about that. I wondered whether you can help me with something rather difficult."

"Go on," Sergeant Scheck encouraged him. "You wouldn't be the first youngster I've helped out of trouble."

He looks friendly enough, Peter thought. This is where we take the bull by the horns again. Aloud he said, "I am afraid my father was arrested in the middle of the night, and I know he's done nothing wrong. But we are Jews, and my mother and I are very worried about him. We must find out where he is. Can you help us with that?"

The smile disappeared from the Sergeant's face. "I'm sorry, you've come to the wrong place," he said. "If your father had been arrested by the regular police for an ordinary offence he would be here. But in fact he isn't. It must have been the Secret Police that came for him, and you'll have to ask at their headquarters. But if you'll take a word of advice, I should leave things alone. The Secret Police don't like anyone interfering. Your father will be all right. I expect he'll soon be back. Sorry I can't do anything for you." And with a friendly nod he turned about and went back up the stairs.

The Headquarters of the Secret Police was not in an imposing building like that of the ordinary police. When the Nazis had first come to power, no one had known where it was. Then, a couple of months later they had arrested a former Mayor of Kolstatt who was known as an active anti-Nazi, and had taken over his flat as their Headquarters. Peter wondered whether he should follow Sergeant Scheck's advice and keep away from the place. No, he thought, if I go I may not do any good. But if I don't go, I shall worry about whether I might have helped by going. And I'll go on worrying until Dad comes home.

So he walked out into the bright summer's day again and made straight for the Secret Police Headquarters. He knew that the place to which he was now going was the one most feared and hated by the people of Kolstatt. He had heard adults talk of it in hushed tones and noticed how they looked round furtively when they mentioned it in case someone might be listening. Still, he thought, I've been lucky twice today, maybe my luck will hold out to the end. I can't give up now, so close to the end of my search.

In a few minutes he arrived outside an ordinary apartment house, just like the one he lived in himself. The only thing which made this one special in a rather sinister way was a small board outside the front door which said simply:

SECRET STATE POLICE—FIRST FLOOR

So this was the dreaded *Gestapo*, as the Germans called it from its German initials. Peter climbed the flight of stairs to the first floor, reminding himself all the time that they couldn't really do him any harm, as he wasn't even quite fourteen. Still, he was far from happy as he went through the open front door of the flat.

He looked around. There were no notices to tell him in which room he should ask. It was clear that the general public didn't normally come in here to inquire. Once again he summoned up his courage, opened the door nearest to him, and entered a room in which there were two large tables. One was covered with stacks of files. At the other table two men in civilian clothes were looking through a pile of private letters and photographs. They both looked at Peter as soon as he opened the door and seemed annoyed at the interruption.

"What do you want in here, boy?" the taller one of them snapped at him. "Can't you read? Don't you know this is the *Gestapo*?"

"I expect you want the Bergs," said the shorter one a little less aggressively. "They're on the next floor up. Run along and leave us alone."

"No, please, sir," Peter said timidly. "I did want the Secret Police. Could you . . ."

"Well I never . . .!" the unpleasant tall man interrupted Peter. "The infernal insolence! Fancy just walking into this office as if we were the Income Tax or something! If we're going to be overrun by schoolboys now, perhaps we'd better open a Kindergarten, eh? Ha, ha, ha!" He laughed ghoulishly at his own joke. "Anyway, who the devil are you?"

In spite of his confusion, Peter remembered his little ruse at the Police Headquarters. "I'm Peter Cronheim, and I stopped the runaway tram the other . . ."

The tall man interrupted again. "All right, all right, we know all about that. Your friend Schulz told us before we sent him on his next job. That still doesn't alter the fact that you're just a little Jew-boy, does it? I think you've got a nerve coming in here! And you still haven't told us what you want now. Well?"

"I wondered whether you could please tell me where my father is," Peter said in a very small voice.

The tall man broke into a fit of laughter as if Peter had just told him a marvellous joke. "Ha, ha, ha! He must think we're the Railway Information Office." Suddenly his face changed and he shouted at Peter in a fury, "Now get out of here before I kick you out!"

By now Peter didn't need much encouragement to leave.

He ran down the stairs as if the devil was after him. When
he reached the sunlit street he didn't stop running until he
had turned the corner, and then only after he had looked
round to make sure that no one was following him.

CHAPTER 9

The Ship

It was a sad Peter who arrived in front of his house a few minutes later. He had been out all the morning but he had not found his father. He hated to disappoint his mother, but what else could he do now? Perhaps he should go and ask Uncle Martin. He looked at his watch. It was lunch time.

If he didn't go home and tell his mother how he had fared she would be worried about him as well as about his father. Not that he wanted to go home for lunch: he wasn't the least bit hungry. Nevertheless, he decided it would be best to return to the flat.

He climbed the two flights of stairs slowly. His failure had made him weary and downhearted, and he wanted to delay as long as he could the moment when he would have to tell his mother about the morning's events.

At last he stood in front of the door to their flat. He rang the bell, saw an eye glance at him through the little spyhole and watched the door open.

For a moment he couldn't believe his eyes.

"Dad!" he almost shouted. "Are you back? I've been all over town looking for you!" He rushed forward and gave his father a big hug—something he hadn't done for many years, because he thought himself too old for it.

"I've just come back," his father said, "and I'm glad you've returned too. Your mother has told me what you set out to do this morning, and we've both been very worried about you. But now come in and tell us where you've been."

Peter started at once to tell his parents about his visit to the local Police Station.

"Would you believe it," his mother said, when he mentioned Christine's policeman husband, "isn't the world a small place! I always said Christine's friend looked a nice boy. If there were more Germans like him we shouldn't be in this trouble now."

"Let me tell you the rest," Peter said, and went on describing every detail of his morning's adventures.

When he had quite finished, he looked up and then, suddenly, remembered what he had forgotten: "And how did you get on, Dad?" he asked quickly. "I should have asked you first really. Are you all right?"

"Yes, thank goodness," his father answered. "But I won't pretend to you that I wasn't frightened at times last night and this morning. I was taken to the Secret Police Headquarters, where you went last. There a whole gang of unpleasant men took turns asking me hundreds of questions non-stop. They were trying to catch me out and make me say something or other. I've no idea what it was. Anyway, as I hadn't done anything wrong I didn't say anything they wanted to hear. So they got tired of me in the end and sent me home. I must have left just before you came, and that horrible man who chased you out knew all the time exactly where I was."

With his father restored to him, Peter's appetite very soon returned too, and he then managed to eat a hearty meal.

"Dad," he asked afterwards, "do you think I'll be able to go abroad now that the Secret Police have our letters with all the addresses from Belgium?"

"I wish I knew, Peter," his father answered. "I'll certainly make fresh inquiries, as I can't see things changing for the better here. I should have listened to your Uncle Martin earlier. He always said that life would get impossible for us if the Nazis came to power."

"Oh, damn the Nazis!" Peter shouted. "I wish I'd been born somewhere else!"

He went to his room, shut the door behind him, and having made sure that no one had followed him, he pulled out a drawer in his desk. There, at the back, was an old envelope. He took it out and opened it. Inside were the broken remains of his little glass dog. He looked at them for a long time with a sense of foreboding. Then he pulled himself

up sharply, and swept them quickly into his waste-paper
basket.

A few more weeks passed, and the summer holidays began.
The terror he had felt when his father was taken for questioning was fading behind the day-to-day routine of life. However, in the last few months, Peter had become much more
concerned with grown-ups' affairs, and he always studied the
newspaper when it arrived in the morning. It was because of
this that he discovered an exciting notice:

"BRITISH WARSHIP TO VISIT KOLSTATT.
H.M.S. *Drake* due next week."

To Peter this spelled romance. Germany had been allowed
only a very small navy after her defeat in the 1914—18 war.
In all his life Peter had seen only one German warship, a
destroyer. He had read all about the famous British Navy,
and he imagined himself holding long conversations in English with the sailors. They would discuss battles and fascinat-
ing details of naval history.

On Sunday afternoon at Oma's he announced his intention
to go down to the river when the *Drake* was due and to
watch her arrival.

"May I come too?" Aunt Teresa asked.

"Yes, of course," Peter answered. "I didn't think you'd
be interested."

"Oh yes," said Aunt Teresa, "there are three things I have
to find out most urgently about this ship."

"Why, Aunt Teresa, I didn't know you spied on the British
Navy!"

Aunt Teresa's eyes twinkled, as they always did when she
was about to make one of her funny remarks. "First, I have
to see whether the sailors in the *Drake* are as smart as those
in the *Kolstatt*. Second, I want to know whether I am getting

too deaf to hear the *Drake's* siren; and third, I should like to beg a free lift to Heringsbeck when the *Drake* goes back."

"Oh, Auntie, you're impossible!" said Peter. "But it'll be nice if you'll come with me."

And so, one morning that week, they both went to the river. When they reached the street which ran along the top of what had once been Kolstatt's fortifications they could see the river down below. It was a colourful scene. All the boats had their flags flying and the river was covered with motorboats full of sightseers. Little clusters of people were lined up all along the quayside, except for a stretch in the centre which was roped off and surrounded by a line of flagpoles flying alternately the German swastika flag and the British Union Jack.

Peter looked around him. There was a big crowd at the top lining the wide road in front of the Town Hall and the museum and the other buildings that made up the familiar skyline. All the buildings had huge red flags hanging from them. These had the familiar black swastikas in a white circle, and amongst them there were also a few British flags.

"I hope the British won't think we're all Nazis," Peter said to Aunt Teresa. "It looks like it with all these swastikas."

"Pardon?" Aunt Teresa asked. "You know you have to speak up when you talk to me."

Peter leant over to speak nearer to Aunt Teresa's ear. "Sorry, I can't shout what I said just now, or we might both be arrested." He continued whispering straight into her ear. "I said I hope that, with all these flags, they don't think we're all Nazis."

"Quite so," Aunt Teresa answered. "That's the fourth reason why I want to see this ship. I should like to explain to one or two of the crew that there are all sorts of different Germans, even Jewish ones, and . . ."

"Look, Auntie," Peter interrupted, "there she comes!"

A murmur of excitement rose from the crowd in the street, for round a bend in the river there now appeared first the bow and presently the whole length of the biggest warship many of the young inhabitants had ever seen. She was only a cruiser, but as she approached the little steamers which had taken Peter to the seaside so many times, Peter could see that she dwarfed every other boat in sight.

Slowly, majestically, and without effort, the *Drake* floated towards the space on the quayside where the notables of the town, and the flags, were waiting for her. One last spurt of her propellers in reverse brought her to a stop a few yards from the side. A whistle blew from her bridge, a rope shot out from her bow, and one from her stern at the same moment. Both were caught on the quayside by several pairs of well-practised hands. A military band in the enclosure down below struck up the British national anthem, followed by "Deutschland über alles" while the cruiser made fast and all the boats blew their hooters in salute.

"Let's go home now," Aunt Teresa said. "We can come back in the afternoon when the ship is open to the public."

Peter agreed enthusiastically. Aunt Teresa had a soft spot for ships, and on occasions like this he liked very much to be with her.

They returned in the afternoon and joined the queue of sightseers which shuffled slowly nearer and nearer to the ship. At last it was their turn, and Peter followed Aunt Teresa up the gangway.

As soon as they set foot on board, Aunt Teresa turned round to Peter and said, "There you are, now you're on British soil."

"I hadn't thought of that," Peter admitted. "How exciting!"

Peter had never in his life heard English spoken by an Englishman. Now he saw little groups of sailors all over the boat chatting among themselves and discussing the visitors they had on board. Peter would have loved to take part in a conversation with one of them so that he could practise his school English, but with such a crowd on board there was no question of stopping. They were ushered along a pre-arranged route which led right round the ship. The traffic was all one way right up to the far end where a second gangway was ready for them and a tall British sailor with a fixed smile on his face called out, "This way, please; this way off; this way off please, this way . . ."

By this time Peter was nearly bursting with the need to speak English to someone. "Thank you very much," he said to the sailor, fully expecting to be drawn into a long conversation. But the sailor didn't even hear him, and went on with his patter: "This way, please, this way off . . ."

Before dinner the next day when Peter's mother was in the kitchen, Peter put his head round the door. "I'm rather hungry, Mother," he said. "Is dinner nearly ready?"

"It will be in about a quarter of an hour," his mother answered. "I wonder whether you'd run round the corner to the baker and bring some bread for the soup? I'll be ready by the time you're back."

"Oh, lovely!" Peter exclaimed. "Then it's pea soup with toasted bread squares! Yes, I'll get you the bread for it right now." And with that he was half-way down the stairs.

He crossed the road, passed the taxi-rank opposite, turned a corner and ran on the hundred yards to the baker's shop. To his surprise and delight when he got inside he saw a British naval officer who had evidently just bought some pastries. He couldn't speak any German, but just pulled a handful of coins out of his pocket and let the baker's wife pick out the right ones. Then, with a smile and a wave of his hand he turned to leave the shop.

"Good-bye, sir!" Peter called out in his best school English.

The officer turned back and beamed at Peter. "Good-bye, young man," he said, and left the shop.

"Aren't these Englishmen charming!" the baker's wife said to her husband when the officer had gone.

"Yes," the baker answered. "And I hope they think the same of us. It's so important for the new Germany that foreigners should like us and trust us."

Peter bought his bread and started on his way home. When he came to the taxi-rank opposite their house he saw the British officer again. He was asking one of the taxi-drivers something in English which the taxi-driver couldn't understand.

"No speak English," the taxi-driver kept on repeating, shaking his head helplessly. This was Peter's chance to practise his English at long last, and he boldly stepped forward.

"Please, Sir Officer," he said—for he was used to addressing everyone in Germany by their title, "the taximan does not speak English. Can I help you, sir?"

The officer looked amused. "I'm so glad someone in this town speaks English," he said to Peter. "I was only trying to get this taxi-driver to direct me back to my ship."

"I will tell you," Peter said, full of importance. "You must turn left at the corner and follow the lines of the street railway . . ."

"You mean the tram-lines?" the officer asked.

"Yes, excuse me, I forgot the word," Peter continued.

"The tram-lines go down to the River Koll where your ship is."

"Thank you very much," the officer said. "Now tell me, where did you learn to speak English so nicely?"

"I learn English at school since four years already," Peter answered.

"I am delighted to hear it," the officer said. "Have you been on board my ship?"

"Yes, sir," Peter answered. "It is marvellous. But I could not speak to anyone in English because there were such many peoples."

The officer smiled again. "You mean, 'so many people', don't you?"

Peter blushed. "I am sorry, my English, it is not very good, but I learn more all the time."

"I am sure you do, young man," the officer said. "All you need is some practice. How would you like to come and visit me on board when there aren't so many people? You can have a really good look round then and talk English to all the sailors."

Peter was almost beside himself with joy. "That would be very fine! Please may I come really?"

"Certainly you may. We'll be here for another week. Just ask your parents to write me a note to say when you are coming. And by the way, what's your name?"

"Peter Cronheim, sir."

"That's funny, I have a boy at home whose name is Peter, and he's just about your age too. I'm Lieutenant Taylor, and I hope to see you on board one day soon."

"Thank you very much, sir."

"Good-bye, Peter, and don't forget to ask your parents to write to me."

As if he would! As Lieutenant Taylor walked towards the

corner to follow the tram-lines as directed, Peter charged across the road and up the stairs two at a time like one possessed. He rang the bell so hard that his mother came racing to the door to see what was the matter.

"My goodness, Peter, whatever is the matter with you?" she said. "Don't tear the bell right off! There isn't a fire, is there?"

"No, Mother, but you'll never guess what happened just now," Peter said.

"Well?" his mother asked a little impatiently, because she was right in the middle of getting the dinner.

"I just met a British naval officer, and he invited me to visit him on board the *Drake*," Peter said breathlessly.

"Who put you up to that story? Aunt Teresa?" his mother asked.

"No, Mother, it's really true," Peter said. "Why don't you grown-ups ever believe anything unexpected?"

His mother still wasn't impressed. "All right then, you can tell your father about it at dinner."

Peter's favourite pea soup with toasted bread squares was wasted on him this time. He hardly noticed what he was eating while he told his father the whole story of his meeting with Lieutenant Taylor.

"He certainly sounds a very kind man," his father said when Peter had finished. "I think we should write and ask him here for an evening. It'll make a nice break for him. I remember how we used to love visiting civilian homes during the war. Service life can be very dull."

Peter was delighted. Not in his wildest dreams had he imagined that he would be under the same roof with a real Englishman. "When can he come?" he asked his mother.

"Let's ask him for Friday evening. Then he can meet some of the family as well."

"May I stay up with you?" Peter asked anxiously.

His father smiled. "I think you'll have to," he said. "There may not be anyone here who knows enough English to entertain him."

CHAPTER 10

The Visitor

Peter would not allow his parents to post their letter of invitation to Lieutenant Taylor. He insisted on taking it in person and marched down to the quayside with it. This time there were no crowds. A policeman stopped him when he reached the entrance to the enclosure round the ship.

"No visiting today," he said.

"I know," Peter answered. "I have to deliver a letter."

"Let me see it then," said the policeman.

With a flourish, Peter produced his letter.

The policeman, who knew no English, carefully studied the address. "Who's it for?" he asked.

Peter pulled himself up to his full height and answered, "It's for Lieutenant Taylor, one of the officers on board the *Drake*."

The policeman looked impressed. "You'd better hand it to one of their sailors," he said, waving in the general direction of the landing stage.

"Thank you," Peter said and passed through. There was a sailor on guard at the bottom of the gangway and Peter went up to him.

"Would you please give this letter to Lieutenant Taylor?" Peter said to him in English. It sounded easy and natural, but he had in fact been repeating this sentence to himself ever since he left home.

"Certainly," the sailor replied. "Are you waiting for an answer?"

This question caught Peter unawares. It had not occurred in his imaginary conversation. "P-pardon?" he stuttered.

"Are you waiting for an answer?" the sailor repeated more slowly.

"Oh—yes, please," Peter said, having collected his wits and thinking that this would be as good a way as any of staying near the ship a little longer.

The man passed the letter on to another sailor further up the gangway. While Peter waited he had a good look at the only piece of Britain on which he had ever set foot. In spite of her size, the cruiser looked graceful and modern. Half a dozen men were standing in cradles hung on the side putting another coat of shiny grey paint on the ship. Up on deck there were about twenty sailors doing physical jerks. "Up, up, up, up, up!" the instructor called out, and up came their arms in unison as if they were determined to reach to the sky. I wonder whether they like gymnastics any more than I do, Peter thought to himself.

"Hello there, Peter," an English voice interrupted his thoughts. "Come along up a minute!"

Peter looked up and there was Lieutenant Taylor calling

him from the top of the gangway. The moment Peter saw him he realized that this was exactly what he had wanted to happen and why he had decided to bring the letter himself.

After a triumphant look towards the German policeman at the entrance to the enclosure, Peter turned and walked up the gangway.

"Good-day, Sir Officer," he called out to Lieutenant Taylor when he arrived at the top.

"Good morning, Peter," Lieutenant Taylor replied. "It was very kind of your parents to invite me. Would you please thank them for me and tell them I'll be delighted to come tomorrow evening?"

"Yes, I will tell them," Peter said in his stilted schoolboy English.

"And since you are here," the officer continued, "have you enough time at the moment to let me show you round the ship properly, as I promised?"

Even if he had been in the greatest hurry imaginable, Peter would not have refused this offer. "Yes, I would like that very much indeed," he said.

For the next hour, Peter was in a new world. He went up and down innumerable stairs and ladders, peeped into scores of cabins and out of dozens of bull's eyes. He inspected the biggest engine room he had ever seen, and he tapped out a message in morse in the wireless operator's room. He stood on the bridge, marvelled at the size of the bow with its gun turret, and saw how small the *Kolstatt* looked tied up a few yards further down the quayside. He listened to Lieutenant Taylor's running commentary in English without difficulty, and, almost without noticing it, found himself asking questions in English.

At length they were back at the gangway.

"Well," Lieutenant Taylor asked, "how did you like your conducted tour?"

Peter hesitated for a moment, searching for an adjective which would really express his delight. "It was very beautiful," he answered at last.

Lieutenant Taylor smiled at Peter's effort. "Yes," he said, "she's a very beautiful ship. I'm proud of her. Now, run along home, Peter, and don't forget to thank your parents for their invitation. I'll see you all tomorrow evening."

"Thank you, Sir Officer," Peter said, "and good-bye!"

In typical German fashion he held out his hand for the officer to shake. This foreign gesture took Lieutenant Taylor by surprise. He was just in the middle of waving his hand at Peter, and he quickly had to drop it to shake hands instead. He couldn't help laughing heartily at this funny situation.

"You know, Peter," he said, "if you and I see much more of each other, you'll become a perfect little Englishman and I will adopt some of your German habits."

They shook hands and Peter turned round and bounced down the gangway. He felt happier than he had done for a long time, in fact since the day when he had been due to go to the Town Hall to collect his reward for stopping the runaway tram.

When he arrived at home, his mother asked, "You were out a long time, Peter. Whatever happened to you?"

Peter suppressed a smile and said as seriously as he could, "I've been to Great Britain, Mother."

"What's the boy talking about?" his father wanted to know from behind his newspaper.

"Well, Dad, it's easy," Peter continued. "I've just spent an hour on British soil."

"You mean Lieutenant Taylor showed you round the *Drake*?" his mother inquired.

"That's right, Mother," Peter answered. "It was wonderful, and all the time he was speaking English and I answered him all right."

"Well done, Peter," his father said. "For people in our position, who don't know where we'll end up, the more languages we know the better."

"Dad," Peter said more thoughtfully. "I wish I could go to England."

"My dear boy," his father answered, "I should be only too happy if I thought you could go to the country of liberty, where a man is judged by what he is, and not by where he comes from or to what religion he belongs. But I don't know anyone in England, and it is impossible to send you to a place where we have no friends or relations who can start you off at school or in a job."

"Let's come down to earth again, shall we?" Peter's mother interrupted the conversation. "You haven't told us yet whether Lieutenant Taylor is coming tomorrow."

"Oh, sorry, Mother, he specially asked me to thank you for your invitation, and he said he would be delighted to come."

In most Jewish families all over the world, Friday evening, the beginning of the Jewish Sabbath, is a special occasion. The Friday evening following Peter's visit on board the *Drake* was even more special for the Cronheim family, for they were at the same time preparing for their first British visitor.

They did not keep many of the Jewish practices, but on most Fridays Peter and his father went to welcome the Sabbath at the service in their synagogue. The inside of the synagogue was not unlike that of a church, with two main differences; there was a gallery running round the walls where the women sat separately from the men, and, instead of taking their hats off, all the men kept them on when they entered. Where the altar would be in a church, there was the Ark, a kind of cupboard with a lavishly embroidered curtain in front, and in this were kept the books of the Bible written on the same old scrolls that the Jews had had for many centuries before the Germans—or the English for that matter —had even learnt to write.

There was no feeling of awe in the synagogue. People came in happily, to find a refuge from the cares of daily life and to remember that their own troubles were small and temporary compared with the long and often sad history of their people.

Soon the organ struck up a cheerful tune, in which the choir and the Cantor joined. The Sabbath, so the Rabbi had explained to Peter in scripture lessons, was greeted by the Jews like a bride at a wedding. That was why Peter liked the Friday evening service best of all. Even so, it seemed to last much longer than usual today, for he was impatient to get home in case Lieutenant Taylor arrived. He didn't even play his game of trying to spot Fräulein Zopp, his piano teacher, who led the sopranos in the choir.

When the service was over, they all filed past the Rabbi and the Cantor to wish them "*Gut Shabbes*" (a happy Sabbath), and made their way out. Peter set a much faster pace home than he did on other Fridays.

His father smiled. "You know, this is all wrong, hurrying like this," he said. "Didn't you learn in Scripture classes what the sages said about going to the synagogue?"

"Yes, Dad," Peter answered. "I know we're supposed to hurry when we go to a service to show how anxious we are to go to the House of God, and to go home slowly after-wards, to show how reluctant we are to leave it. But then in those days they didn't have British naval officers to dinner, did they?"

"No," his father answered, "not British ones, but quite likely Persian, or Greek, or Roman ones. Don't forget that our history goes back a long way, and people haven't altered all that much."

Just as they arrived at their front door, they heard an English voice call out from a few yards behind them, "Hello, Peter! Good evening, Mr. Cronheim!"

Lieutenant Taylor had come just at the right time and they all three went up to the flat together. Peter's mother came into the hall to meet them as Peter's father unlocked the door.

"*Gut Shabbes*, Mother," Peter called out to her. "Meet Lieutenant Taylor. He arrived just as we were coming in."

"How do you do, madam," the officer said in English. "I'm very pleased to make the acquaintance of the mother of my bright young friend here."

Peter's mother looked at him puzzled. "I'm sorry," she said in German, "I don't speak English . . ." and then suddenly remembering a few words of pidgin English she had heard somewhere many years ago, she added, "Sorry, nix English."

Lieutenant Taylor laughed and turned to Peter. "Tell your mother," he said, "she needn't worry. I'm sure with the help of your English and all our arms and legs for sign language we shall do very well."

When Peter translated this, they all laughed and if they were worried before about how to entertain an English visitor, they had now got over it.

"Come straight into the dining-room," Peter's mother said. "Dinner is ready."

Peter's father opened the door for Lieutenant Taylor and they all walked in.

There were two candles lit on the dining-table, as was the custom on Friday evening, and in front of Mr. Cronheim's seat was something under a red velvet cover which was richly embroidered with gold thread in the form of the Star of David and some Hebrew letters.

"Lieutenant Taylor turned to Peter in surprise, "Is all this in my honour?" he asked.

"No," Peter replied, smiling, "our Jewish Sabbath starts tonight. We always have candles for it, and before dinner my father will say the benediction over bread and wine. That's the bread under the cover there," he continued. "Excuse us, while we put our hats on."

Lieutenant Taylor watched while Peter's father poured out some wine into all their glasses, raised his glass and intoned the benediction over the wine in Hebrew. They all drank some, and then Peter's father removed the cover from the bread and said another benediction. He broke pieces off and they all ate a piece each. After that, Peter took the hats outside and they sat down to their usual Friday evening dinner. The main course was always fish, usually with white sauce and often with rice and capers. So it was this evening, and Peter enjoyed his first meal at the same table with an Englishman.

When they had finished, Peter's father recited the thanksgiving prayer which Jews say after meals. Then Peter's mother cleared the dishes, and Lieutenant Taylor, Peter and his father went into the sitting-room.

"You know, Peter," Lieutenant Taylor said as they settled down in their easy chairs, "it had never occurred to me until I came here this evening that you and your family might be Jewish."

Peter's face fell. "Oh," he said, looking embarrassed, "I should have told you, but I forgot. Maybe you wouldn't have wanted to come?"

"Good Lord, no!" Lieutenant Taylor answered. "I am

not a Nazi, I'm an Englishman! It doesn't make any difference to me what your religion is. That is why I never even
thought of it before. My father was a clergyman, and he
taught me to regard the Jewish people with the highest respect.
After all, it is the Jewish Bible which is at the root of Christian life, and we all pray to the same God."

This would no doubt have led to a long discussion on
religion, had not the door bell rung just then.

"I hope you won't mind, Sir Officer . . ." Peter said, but
Lieutenant Taylor interrupted him.

"Just call me Mr. Taylor, Peter," he said. "We are not so
keen on titles as you are in this country. Remember, whatever our rank, we are still ordinary human beings first and
foremost, especially when we're off duty."

"I hope you won't mind—er—Mr. Taylor," Peter started again self-consciously, "but on Friday evenings we usually have the family at our house, and I think they are just starting to arrive."

"Why should I mind?" the officer asked. "Indeed, I am delighted at the chance of being able to meet some German people at home."

"German Jewish people," Peter corrected Lieutenant Taylor politely. "Some German people are like us, but some are very, very different these days."

"Yes, so I know from our newspapers," Lieutenant Taylor said thoughtfully, "but I must say I never realized for one moment how much this affects your outlook. It makes me rather sad to think that decent, charming people like yourselves . . ."

Here they were interrupted again, for now the door to the sitting-room opened and in came Peter's Oma with Aunts Lucie and Teresa, followed by Uncle Martin and Aunt Katie.

There was a long session of mutual greetings, introductions in German, English and a mixture of both, and an interminable series of handshakes of everyone with everyone else. They all settled down in a wide circle round a table, as was the custom in Germany where houses have no open fireplaces. Although the table was round, it became clear at once that the head of the table was where Lieutenant Taylor sat. All heads were turned to him, and according to the amount of English Peter's relations knew, each face had a strained or less strained expression.

Uncle Martin had been a prisoner of war in England towards the end of the First World War and had learnt quite a lot of English. He therefore sat down next to Lieutenant Taylor on one side, while Peter and his father sat on his other side. The three men and Peter kept up a lively conversation while Aunt Lucie, who had visited England as a young girl, gave the ladies a running commentary in German about the subjects they were discussing.

"Do you know Bilscombe, Lieutenant?" Uncle Martin asked. "It's a little village in Lincolnshire, where our prison camp was during the last war."

"I don't actually know it," Lieutenant Taylor answered, "but my wife comes from Lincoln. What was it like there?"

"The people were very friendly to us," Uncle Martin answered. "That was a big surprise, because we were enemies then. We went out and worked on the nearby farms. That is when I learnt English. After that I read many books about England. One day I hope I may go and visit your country again."

"I hope you may be able to do that," Lieutenant Taylor said happily. "You would find quite a few changes, I'm sure, but all in all we are still the same. Why don't you come with your wife for your summer holidays this year? My wife and I would be delighted to put you up for a little while."

Uncle Martin smiled wistfully. "I wish that were possible," he said. "Unfortunately although your people haven't changed much since the war, ours have. The Nazis don't allow ordinary people to go abroad as a rule, except to a few countries of which they approve. And even then they don't allow you to take enough money with you, because they don't like to think that their good German money is being wasted on holidays abroad. And if you're Jewish as we are, they are doubly suspicious."

"Suspicious of what?" Lieutenant Taylor asked.

"Suspicious of our plans. We might, for instance, go abroad in order to try and smuggle out some of our money or valuables. Then, if the Nazis finally drive us out penniless, as they are threatening to do to us Jews, at least we have saved a small part of our possessions. Or we may pretend to go on a holiday abroad, and simply not come back to Germany . . ."

"Yes," Lieutenant Taylor interrupted, "I've read about this sort of thing in the newspapers, but I really don't quite understand it. If I want to leave my country while I'm not actually in the forces, I just obtain a passport and go where I like. Why should any government be interested in keeping me at home?"

"For two reasons mainly," Uncle Martin answered. "First you may make a good soldier if it should come to a war again —and remember, the Nazis think that war is glorious, and that we must all be ready for it at any time. Secondly, if you are too old to be a soldier, you must be made to work for Germany in order to make her strong and ready for a war."

"That isn't a very pleasant prospect for your people, Mr. Cronheim," Lieutenant Taylor said thoughtfully.

"Certainly not," Mr. Cronheim said. "It's like being imprisoned in a house which may at any moment be set on fire by some madmen. However, I always say that it doesn't matter for my generation. We have survived a war, a revolution, the loss of all our money in the inflation, and the arrival of the Nazis in power. No doubt we shall also survive the Nazis."

Uncle Martin frowned. "I'm not so sure of that as you are. But then you always call me the pessimist of the family. I can't see any way out of this except death and destruction, certainly for all of us Jews, and maybe even for many of our fellow-Germans."

"Really, Martin," Oma interrupted the conversation in German when she had heard from Aunt Lucie what was being said, "you shouldn't talk like that in front of the boy. You'll give him nightmares with your gloomy forebodings. Remember he's only a child."

"He would be at any other time," Uncle Martin defended

himself. "But in these times of danger children grow up more quickly and take on responsibilities above those that are normal for their age."

Peter listened wide-eyed to the grown-ups. It struck him that Uncle Martin was right. He had grown up enormously in the last nine months. While the adults continued their English-German conversation, his mind wandered back to his last birthday in the autumn. At that time the most important fact in his life had been the bicycle he had been given. Since then so much had happened: there had been the election, in which he had helped, without success as it proved. His father had lost his job, and his best friend had died with his whole family. He had stopped a tram from crashing and received very little credit for it, merely because he happened to be Jewish. Their flat had been searched by the Secret Police, and his father had been taken away for questioning. Most of his neighbours now looked upon him as a second-rate citizen, someone who, being Jewish, must be bad by nature. And worst of all, there was this dreadful uncertainty about his future and that of his family. Would they all be able to get away? Or would he have to go alone? Or would they have to stay and face whatever came? Perhaps the Nazis would burn themselves out and nothing terrible would happen after all? Or . . .

"What do you think of that idea, Peter?" His father's voice startled him out of his thoughts.

"Sorry, I wasn't listening," he said apologetically. "What idea?"

"Lieutenant Taylor has just offered to write to his old school, where his own son Peter is now, and ask whether they would accept you there either free or at a reduced fee which the Nazis might let us send from here. Don't you think that's an excellent idea?"

Peter was suddenly wide awake. "Really?" he almost shouted, jumping up off his chair. "That would be absolutely wonderful! You are very kind, Sir Off . . . I mean Mr. Taylor —will you really do that?"

"Now don't get too excited, Peter." Lieutenant Taylor beamed at him. "This may or may not work. I know my old school is usually very full and they always have a waiting list. But I will certainly write to the Headmaster and explain your position here."

Peter sobered down. From the very first when he started to learn English he had wanted to go to England. Now it might really be going to happen but it was one thing to go there for a holiday and quite another to go and leave his parents behind—perhaps for a very long time. Well, it was best not to think about that. As Lieutenant Taylor had said, it might not work out.

"Lieutenant," Peter's father said, "naturally we should like to know as soon as possible whether Peter may be able to go to England, but would you please not write to your school until you have left Germany?"

"Whatever for?" Lieutenant Taylor asked in surprise.

"Because letters in this country may be read by the Censor, and if it becomes known that we have told you what things are like inside Germany, we may all suffer, and Peter may never get away."

"Oh," Lieutenant Taylor said, "in that case I shall certainly wait the few more days until we leave here, and then . . ."

He was interrupted by the ringing of the telephone. Peter jumped up to answer.

"It's for you, Uncle Martin," he said after a moment.

Uncle Martin went to the telephone. "Dr. Meyer speaking," he said. There was a pause while he listened to the caller. "I'm so sorry about that," he said presently, "but don't worry, I'll be there in twenty minutes or so. Just keep her lying still until I come. She can have some milk to drink if she wants it. Good-bye."

Uncle Martin turned to the family. "I don't want to break this party up, but unfortunately one of my patients has suddenly fallen ill and I shall have to go and see her."

"Have you far to go?" Aunt Katie asked. "And shall I wait up for you or will you be late?"

"I don't think I'll be very late," Uncle Martin answered. "She lives a long way out, just this side of the Buchwald, but I'll take a taxi, and I don't think I'll have to stay there long. Good night, all, and good-bye, Lieutenant, it's been a great pleasure to meet you."

When Uncle Martin had left the room, Lieutenant Taylor looked at his watch. "Dear me," he said, "I'd no idea how the evening's flown. It's time I got back to my ship. I've very much enjoyed meeting you all, and I hope I shall be able to see some of you again one day, maybe in my country. But now you must please excuse me."

With that there started another long round of handshakes, until finally Mr. Cronheim ushered Lieutenant Taylor out of the room.

Then the rest of the family started to break up for the evening. In the general uproar of "Good night" and "Sleep well", and "See you tomorrow", Aunt Teresa's voice made itself heard. Like many people who are hard of hearing she spoke rather loud.

"Funny people, these English," she was saying now. "They call their schoolboys 'Master', and they call their teachers 'Master'. I wonder how they know the difference."

CHAPTER 11

Before Another Birthday

Peter opened his eyes the next morning when his mother called him. As soon as he saw her face, he knew something was wrong again. The thing he hated most about his present life was its terrible uncertainty. You never knew what the next day, or even the next hour, would bring.

"What's wrong, Mother?" he asked anxiously. "It's not Dad again, is it?"

"No, Peter," his mother said in a worried tone, "but it's

nearly as bad. You remember Uncle Martin was called to a patient last night?"

"Yes, Mother."

"Well, it turned out to have been a bogus call, made by some young Nazi hooligans. When he got out of the taxi and walked up the long, narrow footpath to the house, they jumped on him and beat and kicked him until he was unconscious. If the taxi-driver hadn't got worried after an hour or so and started wandering up to the house to see how things were going, Uncle Martin would probably have died of exposure. As it is, the taxi-driver, who was himself a patient of Uncle Martin's, ran him to hospital. It seems that, apart from bruises, he has three broken ribs and is suffering from concussion and shock."

"But, Mother," Peter cried out, "why should anyone want to hurt Uncle Martin?"

"It isn't Uncle Martin in particular that they want to hurt, Peter," his mother explained. "He is the most inoffensive of men, and has spent his whole life making other people better. But he is a Jew, and the Nazis don't like seeing Jews who are decent and popular, because that doesn't fit in with their ideas."

"Mother," Peter said, "I hate it here. Can't we *all* get out? I don't want to have anything to do with the Germans. I think they are wicked."

"I know how you feel, Peter," his mother said, trying to soothe him. "I often feel like that myself, but then I try to remember that our friends the Laumanns upstairs are also Germans, and so is the taxi-driver who took Uncle Martin to hospital last night, and Mr. Senner, whom the Nazis imprisoned, and your school friend Walter Abel. I quite agree with you that it would be nice if we could all just pack up our things and go abroad until the Nazis are finished, but it isn't so easy, as you know. If only Lieutenant Taylor can get you into his old school your father and I will be very happy."

"I wish we could all go together, Mother. If I go, I shall miss you dreadfully."

"I am sure you will, and we'll miss you just as much. Sometimes in life you have to put up with a lesser evil in order to avoid a greater one. I'd rather miss you and know you to be safe, than to have you here miserable, unhappy, and insecure."

"I wonder how soon we shall hear from the school in England," Peter said. "I wish I knew one way or the other."

The next few weeks seemed years to Peter. Nothing happened to make the time go quickly. Every morning he ran to the front door to see whether there was a letter from England. As soon as he was certain that there was none, he scanned the headlines of the *Kolstatt Daily Journal*, to see if anything dreadful had happened. To his relief, there was nothing.

After a time he began to wish the new school term would hurry up and start. At least it would take his mind off things, even if he did have to sit with his remaining Jewish friend apart from the others; and even if some of the boys did call after them "Dirty Jew-boys" and "Jewish pigs, go back to Jerusalem!"

He was allowed to visit Uncle Martin a few times in hospital once he had begun to improve. He had long and serious talks with him and found him much changed. He no longer talked about making people more reasonable and helpful to each other. He had instead adopted a counsel of despair.

"Peter," he said, "get out of here while you are still able. It's too late for my generation, our graves are already dug for us here. At least we must try to save the young ones. I'm sorry that we can't do any better for you. I suppose we have to admit that we've failed, and you will have to make your own life elsewhere."

When Peter was at his Oma's flat one Sunday afternoon in early August, Oma asked him what he would like for his birthday.

"I don't know really," he answered. "I haven't given it any thought. Somehow it doesn't seem half as important to me this year as it did last. I remember how excited I was when I saw my new bicycle. I can't believe that was only eleven months ago. It seems ages!"

Oma looked at him with sad eyes. "A lot has happened since then," she said. "That's why it seems a long time. Poor Peter, they've robbed you of some of your childhood."

Peter looked at her in amazement. He wasn't quite sure what she meant.

As always, Aunt Teresa could be relied on to bring the discussion back to a cheerful level: "I know exactly what you want for your birthday, Peter," she said, her eyes twinkling.

"Well?" Peter asked.

"I'll go straight down to the railway station and buy your present now, in case they sell out."

"Whatever are you talking about, Aunt Teresa?" Peter wanted to know.

"A ticket to London, of course," she said.

Peter was getting more and more short-tempered and irritable. The only thing that still gave him some pleasure was hard physical exercise. As he let off steam, cycling uphill as if pursued by a pack of wolves, or swimming across the lake as if it was shark-infested, he felt that he was getting even with fate. It was now the middle of August, and he had almost given up hope of hearing from Lieutenant Taylor or his school.

One warm sunny morning when he came home from swimming he was so depressed that he didn't even bother to wonder what there was for dinner.

But this time his mother came running to the door to let him in. "Peter," she greeted him excitedly, "I could hardly wait for you to come home. There's a letter here from England. It didn't come till the second delivery. Your father had gone out by then, and I cannot read it. Do have a look!"

Peter almost snatched the letter from her, and translated for her as he read:

"Dear Mr. Cronheim,

We understand from one of our Old Boys, Lieutenant Taylor, whose son is at present at this school, that you would consider sending your son to us if permission can be obtained from your government.

My Board of Governors has agreed that if such permission is obtained we can offer your son a free place.

I shall be glad to hear from you whether you are interested in this offer.

Yours truly,

H. SMITH,

Headmaster."

Peter knew now that this was what he and his parents had set their hearts on. He was their only hope. He looked at his mother swiftly for a moment, then put his arms round her neck and gave her a big kiss.

Just then Peter's father came in.

"What's going on here?" he asked. "Anyone would think you've just been accepted by an English school or something!"

"But, Dad, that's just what it is! Look, here's their letter," Peter cried excitedly.

Peter's father read it through. Peter knew that he too had lost heart lately and had doubted whether they would ever hear any more of Lieutenant Taylor or his school. Peter noticed that his father's relief was tremendous, but even so, he still sounded a note of caution.

"I won't pretend I'm not extremely pleased, Peter," he said. "But we still have a few hurdles to jump. We have to see the authorities and get a passport and permission for you to leave."

"Yes, I know," Peter said more quietly. "I remember we'd nearly reached this stage with the Belgian school to which I should have gone and I'm still here. Oh, Dad, I do want to be lucky this time."

"No one wishes that more than I do, Peter. I shall rest content if I know that my son is safely out of Germany and making a new free life for himself."

"And I shan't be content until I have you both with me," Peter said. "I'll try and make as many friends as I can in England, and I'll tell them all what it's like here, and maybe they'll club together and bring you and Mother over."

"Well, Peter," his mother said, and tears came into her eyes, "I shouldn't put too much faith in that idea. There are half a million of us, and they don't really want us in the other countries without means to maintain ourselves. Let's do first things first. That means you."

Never was a dinner in the family of Cronheim eaten more hastily. There was so much to do before Peter could leave the country, and there was no time to waste. There was no telling what horror the next day might bring.

The local Police Station was the first port of call that afternoon for Peter and his father. The officer there merely said that emigration was not their affair and sent them on to the Central Police Headquarters.

How different this building looked to Peter now! The last time he had been there he had been desperately frightened. This time he was full of hope, and, with him, was his father who, as a lawyer, seemed quite at home in the place. Even the unpleasant policeman inside the entrance door said, "Good afternoon, Mr. Cronheim," quite politely in his shrill voice.

"Good afternoon," Mr. Cronheim returned his greeting. "Do you mind if my son waits here while I do some business upstairs?"

"Certainly," the policeman replied. "You go ahead. I'll see the young man isn't taken away by bandits or the police." And his face broke into the hideous grin that Peter remembered from his last visit.

Silly old fool, Peter thought. Does he take me for a baby? He sat down quietly on the very same bench where he had sat waiting for Sergeant Scheck to arrive. He had been equally hopeful then, but much more frightened.

After what seemed an eternity to Peter, his father returned.

"I've notified the authorities of your intention to leave the country and applied for a passport."

"Does that mean I'll really be able to leave?" Peter asked, barely hiding his anxiety.

"Unfortunately no—not quite yet. The police have to check with the Secret Police that they have no objection, and with the Tax Authorities to make sure you owe no tax. Then we have to apply to the German National Bank for permission for you to 'export', as they call it, your own belongings and ten marks in cash on top of that. Ten marks is barely enough to pay the railway porters and for your breakfast during the journey. Even if you don't pay the porters and go without breakfast you'll still only get twelve shillings for ten marks in England. Therefore we also have to prove that someone will meet you at the other end and pay all your expenses abroad. And while all this goes on, we must fit you out from top to toe for a year or two ahead, since you'll have no money to buy anything once you have left, except what friends may let you have or what you may earn yourself."

Peter's face fell. He had not dreamt that there would be all these complications, even though he had thought for months of the possibility of leaving his home.

If the previous weeks had crawled like snails, the next three weeks flashed by like lightning. There was so much to do! Visits to the photographer for passport photos were followed by fittings at the tailor for new suits and a winter overcoat. There were shopping expeditions and letters to write in English and German. Then the detailed clothing list arrived from the school, and alterations had to be made to clothes already ordered.

In the middle of it all money became short, and in a sudden fit of gratitude to his parents, Peter took his bicycle to a shop and sold it. I shan't need it any more when I've gone, he said to himself, and that's the least I can do to help my parents pay for all the things they have to buy for me.

The one thing Peter enjoyed most of all was a visit to his school. The new term had started, but he didn't have to go to school any more. Instead, one morning, he went to collect his school leaving certificate. He arrived in the middle of a period, and the big building seemed very quiet with all the boys busy inside their classrooms.

He went straight upstairs to the Headmaster's study, as he had been told. He knocked at the door.

"Come in," he heard Dr. Westreich say from inside.

He pushed the door open, and with his head high proudly marched up to the Headmaster's desk.

"Ah, Heil Hitler, Cronheim!" Dr. Westreich said. "I hear you are leaving us."

"Yes, sir," Peter answered simply.

"Well," Dr. Westreich continued, "we are sorry to lose you, for you have been a good pupil, and I think you will grow into a sensible man. I want you to understand that the policy of our glorious government is not against you personally. I know there are good Jews and bad Jews. However, we small individuals can do nothing against history. So I can only wish you all the best in England and hope that this certificate will help you."

Peter wanted to say all sorts of things. He wanted to explain to the Headmaster that it was nonsense to persecute all Jews because some were bad, and that there were plenty of bad Germans too. He wanted to point out that in England people believed that individuals do make history, and that the dictates of one's own conscience are more important than blind obedience. And a lot more besides. But then, he thought if I start a political argument now, I may never be allowed out of the country. So all he said was, "Thank you, sir. Good-bye."

"Heil Hit . . . I mean good-bye, Cronheim!" the Headmaster called after him, for Peter was already half-way out of the door.

At last everything was ready except the clearance from the Secret Police.

Peter hadn't had time to worry until then, but now he became anxious again. What if permission wasn't granted? The thought was too painful to be pursued to its logical conclusion; instead it became a nagging doubt which Peter couldn't shake off for days on end. People like the Goldens had just bolted across the frontier without any documents. If he didn't get permission perhaps that's what he ought to try? But he hadn't heard of any children doing it on their own.

"I think I ought to go and see the Secret Police," Peter's father said one day. "At least I might find out what Peter's chances are."

"Oh no, Dad, don't do that," Peter cried. "I'd much rather wait than have you go to that hateful place for me."

There was a letter in the post the very next morning from the Central Police Headquarters, informing Mr. Cronheim that all formalities having been duly completed, permission had now been granted for his son to leave for England and that his passport could be collected at his convenience.

Later that morning Peter left the Central Police Headquarters with his father. He was as proud as he had been when he was on his way to the Town Hall to meet the Mayor, but this time it wasn't because of something he had done. It was because he was now the owner of a passport with a permit which allowed him to go to England.

"I feel I've cleared the last hurdle, and know I'm winning—just the way I used to feel in the hurdle race at school," Peter said.

Once again his father struck a warning note. "You still have the frontier to cross, Peter."

"But surely, Dad, they can't stop me now, when I have all my papers in order?"

"I hope they won't, but until you are safely on the other side I'm afraid there is always the chance that something might go wrong. I don't want to paint too black a picture, but remember that the Nazi government is a dictatorship and can do what they like. If, overnight, they suddenly decide that no Jews at all shall be allowed out of Germany, then no passport, however valid, would be any use."

"I don't think I could bear it if something stopped me now," Peter said.

"I hope you won't have to," his father said.

Now that most of the worry and bustle were over, Peter had a little time to think. As he began fully to realize his new situation, a strange feeling came over him which he had never known before.

He knew that the next few days would be spent with last minute fittings and purchases, and visiting all his friends and relatives to say good-bye. Then he would board the familiar train to Berlin. There he would take a taxi to another station to go on another train to the German frontier. The train itself would be familiar enough, but this part of the route would be new to him. And after that? It was this unanswered question that made him feel lost and strange. He was due to go to school in England but he had no idea what anything would be like once he had crossed the frontier. His future from a moment in time which he could determine exactly from looking at the timetable of his train was hidden by a blank wall.

He wasn't afraid of this blank wall. He was quite hopeful that behind it lay a friendly country and a future full of opportunity and he was determined to make good use of it. All the same, the fact was that he knew nothing whatever about the new life ahead of him and in this lay the feeling of strangeness and uncertainty.

The earliest date for which they could book reserved seats on the train happened to be Peter's fourteenth birthday.

"Let's leave it till the day after," his mother said, "so that we can celebrate the birthday together."

"Please, Mother," Peter pleaded, "don't let's leave it any later than we have to. What if a new law stopped me on that very day, and I could have gone the day before? I'll tell you what, we'll celebrate my birthday the day before, and then I'll leave on my real birthday."

His mother would have liked to argue, but she didn't.

"All right then," she said. "I suppose if something really went wrong due to that one day's delay I'd never forgive myself."

Having settled the date of departure, Peter now started a new game. It was the game of doing or seeing things "for the last time".

He took his last walk by the River Koll one morning, looking at all the boats, many of which had carried him to the seaside. Odd, he thought, they are moored there quite unconcerned. They don't care whether I'm here or not. They'll still be going to the seaside next week-end, even though I shan't be here to go on them or even to look at them.

He passed the house in which the Secret Police had their headquarters. It still gave him an unpleasant feeling because he knew that he wasn't safe yet. But if all went well, then, in a week's time, he wouldn't have to worry about it any more. At least not for himself. But his parents and relations would still be in danger. Well, maybe he could do something for them all once he had established himself in England. He was certainly going to try.

He went on his way lost in thought, and only looked up when a tram in the middle of the road rang its bell. Out of habit, he glanced at the number painted on the side of the car. "Four-seven-eight," he said to himself. "What do I know about four-seven-eight? Oh, of course, that was the very tramcar that I stopped at the bottom of the hill less than a year ago." Now it had come to say good-bye to him. He looked for the driver, but it was a new young face that he hadn't seen before. Probably a young Nazi, he thought.

It was harder saying good-bye to people. His piano teacher, Fräulein Zopp, burst into a flood of tears.

"I know I shall never see my little Peter again," she sobbed. "I do hope you'll be all right in a strange land!"

Peter would have liked to go and see Walter Abel who had always been so friendly at school, but his parents thought it might not be good for Walter or his parents if a Jew came to their house just before going abroad, so he wrote him a letter to say good-bye.

The family were all invited for Peter's "pretend" birthday, the day before he was due to leave. They came for coffee and cakes in the afternoon, and brought leaving presents by which they would be remembered and which wouldn't add too much to the luggage: Oma brought a new watch, Aunt Lucie and Aunt Teresa a fountain pen and a propelling pencil, Aunt Katie a tie pin. Uncle Martin was well enough again to hobble around on a stick, and he brought a leather wallet.

While they were in the middle of drinking their coffee, Uncle Martin slowly rose from his chair, with the help of his stick, and said, "This may not be the right time to make any speeches, but I just want to say to you, Peter, what I know we all feel today. We are, first and foremost, sad at the thought that for the time being at least we shall lose you. We shall miss you, because you have always helped us to keep cheerful, and it has been a pleasure to have you with us. We also feel proud, because we are going to be so well represented by you in England. And we feel hopeful, because we know that in England you will have a first rate chance to grow into a decent man and to earn a good living in whatever occupation you choose. This is a very hard day for your parents and your grandmother, and I dare say for you, too, Peter. But remember it is also the beginning of something new and exciting, and all of us here have enough faith in you to believe that

you will make a success of your new life. Just one last thing, Peter. Remember us. If it should go from bad to worse with us, remember us as we used to be, a happy and decent family. If things here should become better after all, come back to us, and you will be very, very welcome."

By this time, Peter's mother was crying quietly, and Oma looked at Peter full of sadness. As Uncle Martin slowly groped for his chair and sank into it again, Peter wanted to stand up and say something in return. But a large lump had appeared in his throat, his eyes filled with tears, and he couldn't say a word. After what seemed a very long time, he managed to lean across the table to Uncle Martin and to say simply, "Thank you, Uncle Martin, I won't forget."

Once more, Aunt Teresa lifted every one out of their depression. "Dear me," she suddenly burst out, "I nearly forgot the most important present for our cosmopolitan traveller!" Tears turned to watery smiles as she produced—a man's umbrella. "You'll need this," she said with a straight face. "It always rains in England."

CHAPTER 12

Between Two Worlds

For as long as Peter could remember, he seemed to have been sitting in his corner seat, listening to the rhythmical "rat-a-tat-tat" of the train over the rails, looking out of the window, eating a sandwich or two, and occasionally walking up and down the corridor. The prospect of a long train journey had at first seemed exciting. He had hated saying good-bye to his parents at the station more than he had hated anything else ever before. After that, he began to enjoy the novelty of the first hour or two in the train by himself. But by the time he had changed trains in Berlin and travelled for a few hours in the second train, the whole thing had become dull and dreary.

What a way to spend a birthday, he thought. He closed his eyes and thought about the last one. What a difference! He could remember exactly how he had carefully opened the sitting-room door in Oma's flat and had first caught sight of the bicycle. Poor bicycle! He wondered where it might be now. Perhaps it was still standing in the shop, waiting for someone to buy it. Or perhaps some other boy had just had a big surprise and found it with his birthday presents . . .

The brakes came on again and interrupted his thoughts. He opened his eyes to see how far they had come. Outside, dusk was falling. He had been travelling since early morning, and he knew that he was well on in the west of Germany. Now they were moving again and a station flashed by, too fast for him to read the name, and the train sped on into the gathering darkness.

He knew that in another hour or two he would be at the frontier. The nearer he got to it, the more fervently he wished that he was already on the other side. I do hope it will be all right, he said to himself. I don't know what I'll do if they stop me. But they must let me pass. I've got a valid passport. They must, they must, they must.

He relaxed again. He felt as if he was going through a long, long tunnel. At one end was all his past life, and at the other end nothing that he could distinguish. Then again he imagined himself floating, timelessly, between two worlds, the one he knew and another one which he wouldn't be able to see or imagine until he was actually there. I wonder what Mother and Dad are doing right now, he said to himself. Perhaps they are having supper and looking at the empty place where I used to sit. Oh, how long this tunnel is, we must be nearly there, nearly there, nearly there . . .

"Have your tickets ready, please!"

Peter's heart missed a beat with fright. He had, after all, fallen asleep. A large, amused looking German ticket collector watched him groping in his pocket for his ticket. As he handed it over for yet another series of holes to be punched into it, he asked, "Where are we now, please?"

"We're at the frontier, sonny," the ticket collector said kindly. "I'd get my cases ready for the customs if I were you. Going to London, eh? You lucky boy!"

With that he moved on to the next compartment. Peter climbed on to his seat and started to struggle with his suitcase in order to lower it on to the seat for the customs inspection. While he was pulling at it the door to the compartment was opened again and a sharp voice said behind him, "Passports please!"

Peter's heart sank. This, he knew, was the decisive moment. Abandoning the case, he jumped down from the seat and took his passport from his breast pocket. As he handed it over he looked at the official who owned the sharp voice. He didn't like what he saw. He was a small man, wearing a peaked cap with a swastika badge pinned on it. He had sharp features which matched his voice and a mean look in his eye.

"Cronheim," he mumbled to himself, "Kolstatt to London, let's see now, let's see . . ."

He looked through a little pocket notebook, and after a moment, he looked up at Peter triumphantly.

"You'd better bring your things out and come with me. I want you."

Peter stood completely stunned, as if he had been struck deaf and dumb. He felt the colour go from his face.

"Well, come on," the little man barked, "we haven't got all night!"

This is the end, Peter thought. He felt like a trapped animal watching the hunters approach. Mechanically he climbed back on to the seat, gave a wrench to his heavy suitcase and let it drop to the floor with a thud. He stepped down, picked it up, and followed the Nazi out of the carriage on to

the platform of a dark, deserted looking railway station.

The little man walked briskly along the platform. Following him, Peter struggled with his heavy case, puffing and blowing and wondering all the time whether he ought not to drop the case and run for the frontier. He was sure some people in his position would do that. But he had no idea where the frontier was. By the time he had really thought about it, they had both reached a room which reminded Peter of the local Police Station at Kolstatt.

There was the same desk-like barrier running across the whole width of the room. Behind it was a table with four

chairs, and three men were sitting there playing cards. Peter
thought the fourth chair must be for his horrid little man,
when one of the other three greeted Peter's escort uncere-
moniously.

"Well, look at this, boys! Whatever have you brought in?
Been baby-snatching? Or gone into the kidnapping game?"

"Shut up and read your notes," Peter's escort answered.
"Cronheim, Kolstatt. Page five."

The other man seemed a little surprised. He looked at a
little notebook similar to the one Peter's escort had. After a
moment, which seemed an eternity to Peter, he raised an
amused eyebrow.

"Well?" he said to Peter's escort. "I've read it."

The little man was getting visibly annoyed with his colleague. "Stop playing about. Don't you want him?"

He thumbed through his notebook again, found the place
and recited "Cronheim, Kolstatt. Organizer of local Jewish
lawyers. Under investigation."

"You want to enter your amendments a little more con-
scientiously," the other man said, and now it was his turn to
get annoyed. "Then you'd know that Cronheim was cleared
four weeks ago. Look, it says here, 'delete, now cleared.'
Take the baby back and don't waste our time."

Peter's heart started beating normally again, the colour
came back to his cheeks, and he wasn't the least bit concerned when the unpleasant little man hissed at him. "Now
get back into that train, you lousy little Jew-boy. I don't
want you to miss it, because I don't want you back in
Germany!"

Back in his compartment again, Peter left his suitcase on
the floor. He hadn't the strength to put it up into the luggage
rack. As he slumped down into his seat, he felt a cold sweat
all over his face. He pulled out his handkerchief to wipe it

and, at that moment, the engine gave a whistle, and slowly, slowly, the train began to move. Perhaps he should use his handkerchief to wave good-bye to Germany and everything German. This idea made him want to laugh. Thank God I can laugh again, he thought to himself.

At last I'm safe!

CHAPTER 13

Only a Bad Dream

The cold grey light of early morning showed the outline of the window at the end of the long school dormitory. Peter Cronheim was tossing and turning in his sleep. His dream had taken him back to Germany.

"Brrr-brrr, brrr-brrr, brrr-brrr," went the telephone. Peter ran across the room and lifted up the receiver.

"This is Kolstatt 20805," he said.

"Dad here," answered the voice at the other end. "Tell Oma I won't be in to dinner, please, Peter."

Strange, Peter thought, that voice sounded like my own.

"Why not?" he asked.

"Can't explain now," said the voice, "I have to catch a train to Brussels."

"When will you be back?" Peter asked anxiously, but the voice at the other end had rung off.

He went out into the kitchen to find Oma and deliver the message. Oma wasn't there, but Uncle Martin, without a sign of his recent injuries, was busily packing a large suitcase.

"Dad won't be in to dinner," Peter said to Uncle Martin.

"I know," Uncle Martin replied without looking round and continued his packing.

"What's the matter with everyone today?" Peter asked. "Are you all going away?"

"No, not all," Uncle Martin answered. "Some of us are staying here to die, but you had better follow your father to Brussels."

"Oh no, he won't," said another voice. Peter looked round and behind him in the doorway stood a man whom he knew to be Mr. Schulz, their former lodger, but he looked like Mr. Cohn, Rudi's father, and he was carrying a policeman's helmet under his arm.

"Let me out, I have to go to London," Peter said and tried to push past Mr. Schulz.

"No," he answered, and now he spoke with Mr. Cohn's voice. "We couldn't live in any other country. We must tighten our belts and . . ."

He was interrupted by Lieutenant Taylor who appeared behind him dressed like a Kolstatt tram driver.

"At least send your children out of the country if you won't go yourselves," Lieutenant Taylor said to Mr. Schulz.

The telephone started to ring again. Brrr-brrr, brrr-brrr brrr-brrr . . .

Peter struggled with Mr. Schulz and tried to get out through the door.

"I must answer the 'phone," he shouted. "The Mayor wants to speak to me. Help me, Sir Officer, I must answer the 'phone, I must answer the 'phone, I must . . ." and with one big push he upset Mr. Schulz enough to rush past him into the corridor.

The telephone was still ringing, but Peter couldn't find the living-room. The corridor was that of a train carriage, and it was pitch dark outside the windows. Now the man from the Secret Police Headquarters in Kolstatt came towards him.

"Go and answer that telephone, you lousy little Jew-boy," he hissed.

"But I can't find it," Peter said plaintively.

"Then you'll have to go back to Kolstatt," the man said.

I must jump out of this train, Peter thought, and he tried to open one of the doors. The handle jammed and he couldn't move it. The telephone was ringing continuously now, "brrrrrrrrrrrrrrrrrrrrrrrrr . . ." He felt the man from the Secret Police take hold of his collar.

"Help me, somebody!" Peter shouted. "I can't get out!"

"It's all right. I'll help you, Peter," an English voice said. Peter opened his eyes. Where was he?

"Wake up, and get a move on. The bell's gone. You're in England now, and you'll jolly well have to step on it if you want breakfast!"

Peter sat up. *In England!* Yes, it was true and his new friend Peter Taylor was sitting up in the bed next to his. A great feeling of relief came over him.

Suddenly a pillow landed on his head. He grabbed it and hurled it across the room at Peter Taylor who was now half-way through the door. Peter Cronheim jumped out of bed and chased after him, laughing—into a new, happy day. . . .